I0573624

FAIRCHILD

FAIRCHILD, VOLUME ONE

BLAZE WARD

KNOTTED ROAD PRESS

Fairchild
Fairchild, Volume One

Reviews

It's true. Reviews help. Even a short one, such as, "Loved it!" So please consider reviewing this book (and all of the ones you've read) on your favorite retailer site.

Never miss a release!

If you'd like to be notified of new releases, sign up for my newsletter.

http://www.blazeward.com/newsletter/

Buy More!

Did you know that you can buy directly from my website?

https://www.blazeward.com/shop/

ALSO BY BLAZE WARD

CHAPTER ONE

FAIRCHILD

"RECON ONE, this is Ground Station Beta," the voice coming out of the Science Shuttle's speakers sounded just a little too laconic to Dani, especially for one of the big-brained boffins back at the research station, but Dr. Chike Odille wasn't your normal Planetologist/Geologist. "How's it look up there, Fairchild?"

Dani smiled, alone on her bridge. Nobody on this entire planetary survey crew knew her by anything but the nickname *Fairchild*. And they were probably all too old and stodgy to recognize even that from the days of her crazy, youthful stunts. At least her legacy was insured on the video channels of various colony worlds.

Oh, for the days of teenage rebellion and armchair anarchy.

And she really wasn't that old at thirty-one.

Dani did a quick scan of the consoles and readouts in front of her without taking her gloved hands from the big, off-white flight controller yoke with all the programmed buttons. She looked up and out the front windshield at the gold/pink horizon, then back to the heads-up display.

All systems within tolerance range. Power flowing smoothly to the thrusters keeping the Science Shuttle aloft and stable. Inside, everything was normal in the weirdly beautiful skies of Escudra VI.

Outside, things were threatening to get a little hairy.

Air pressure kept dropping, but humans hadn't been on this planet long enough to really know what the comfortable or safe range should be. And AI's were too expensive to waste down on the surface of a planet.

The one that had been dedicated to the whole planet just sat in orbit and cataloged all the data from lots of little, dumb, automated stations that were dropped and then parachuted into place, like javelins from the sky. But silicon systems had no soul. It took flesh and blood people to get a feel for things on a new planet.

All that smart systems could tell you were probabilities and past experience. No guarantee of future performance, kind of like some of the men she'd known

"Four and One, Beta Station," Fairchild replied crisply. Almost perfect signal, only minor degradation from atmospheric conditions around her.

She knew Chike well enough to appreciate the hint of concern she heard in his voice, but that was a cultural thing. He had grown up on old Earth, where women were still supposed to be sheltered, rather than one of the colonies where everyone was expected to pull their own weight, even the youngest daughter of the richest man on the planet.

At least she had taken up aerial gymnastics and free-gliding as a teenager instead of clothes and makeup, like her older sister, Chloe.

It had made the bodysuit she was wearing look good on her compact form. She was a meter-seven tall and fifty-two kilos of lanky muscle, with blond hair in a pixie cut tucked up under her flight helmet and bright, blue eyes with a hint of gray underneath.

Her navy blue bodysuit emphasized all the right places, with black gloves, boots, and emergency survival belt to complement it, and a single white racing stripe down her right side, over her small breast, and down to her hip. It drew the eye to the places she wanted it drawn.

Dani knew she was trouble just waiting to happen. And she wanted to look it, too.

"Sounds good, Fairchild," Odille replied. "Be careful out there. We're starting to get some really strange readings on the ground radars and monitors."

Dani could see that.

Originally, she had just been flying a quick aerial survey with the Science Shuttle into the general vicinity of a thunderstorm north of Ground Station Beta. It was the sort of thing she had done routinely on two other planetfall missions before this.

Cakewalk, but it paid the bills until she could convince her father to unblock her credit accounts again.

Even he couldn't maintain that level of stubborn forever.

Still, on the other hand, she just had to have gotten her stubbornness from her mother, the much sainted Sìleas, who had been a fashion model before she became the third Mrs. Alphonse Cooper.

Up until now, the flight had been almost mundane and normal outside. There was nothing about Escudra VI to make people nervous. Just another planet, habitable if somewhat dry and arid.

But outside, the air was starting to get *weird*.

That was a scientific term. Dani was sure of it. Even xeno-meteorologists used it from time to time. She'd been there listening, and only mostly drunk.

"Perhaps, dear, we should consider discretion?" a new

voice chimed in from the console in front of Dani. Unlike Chike, this voice had an edge to it, one just the slightest bit this side of vicious, biting sarcasm. "Just this once, mind you. Wouldn't want you to develop a *reputation*, or anything."

Dani scowled at the handheld computer, the Aide that was her Governess. The AI had been her constant companion almost since birth, learning all Dani's foibles and tricks and duly reporting them to Dani's parents. At least until she'd threatened to reprogram the damned thing or sell it to a street urchin.

"It's fine, Eleanor," Dani growled back at the handheld comm secured into the dash-port, before switching to honey. "I would have thought you would have developed a taste for adventure by now."

"Unlike you, dearie, I was programmed for sanity," Eleanor huffed in a scold.

Early to bed, early to rise, makes a man healthy, wealthy, and wise, as the wise, old scientist Franklin used to say.

…and boring as hell.

Besides, the best part was just about upon them. This was what got Dani out of bed in the morning.

On the very edge of her scanners, Dani could see the anvil of the greatest, most awesomely huge storm head she could ever remember beginning to turn, to fall as it reached that final stage of life.

On Earth, nasty ones got to fifteen or maybe twenty thousand meters at most before they collapsed in on themselves. Escudra VI was a larger world, but had about the same gravity as Earth. The top of that beast was easily forty thousand meters, maybe fifty, depending on the topography over there as the weather front climbed a low mountain range and began to transform itself into bottled anger.

She couldn't remember exactly where the line of the ridge

ran, and didn't care enough to bring up the local topographical radar display right now.

It was enough to anticipate what was coming next.

She hoped that the folks back at Beta were getting as good a view of this as she was.

The feeling in her stomach was almost the same as when some cute boy or girl in a bar first spotted Dani, and screwed up the courage to walk over and talk to her. That fine edge of just how far she could tease, how thin she could cut her odds, before she either scared them off or just surrendered and let herself be well and truly ravished.

A good ravishing every now and again kept the senses sharp and the reflexes tight. She was living proof.

Out there, she could feel it. The Science Shuttle's controls started to get a little mushy as the air turned weird and the wind began to race.

On Earth, the best place to experience those winds was right about a kilometer and a half off the deck.

That was where the outflow boundary would be the roughest, the strongest. The squirreliest.

Here, she let her instincts lead her to a spot right around four kilometers up where she could thread the needle.

The best whitewater you could find in the sky.

Dani turned the Shuttle's nose into the wind and accelerated.

Not much. Just a couple of strokes with the paddles to establish a path down that massive river.

There. The gust front was running.

The storm had died at the very peak of the ridge as it moved and that anvil was now a column of hot air roaring straight down on this side of the ridge and slamming into the ground.

There was no virga here, no column of precipitation. Just lightning.

Escudra VI was a dry world. It had been wet once, but that was so long ago that the boffins thought they might be able to establish when the Elder Race had disappeared, just by figuring out how much the terraforming had failed on certain worlds humans had found when they started exploring the galaxy.

So right now, there was no water to cushion the fall of that air. Nothing to absorb the heat and dissipate the energy that had climbed so high into the mid-afternoon sun.

It was going straight down like a cliff-diver.

Dani tasted the power as the air on the backside of the storm had nowhere to go but downhill as well, doubling the flow that was coming right at her and the blunt bow of the *Qunsahr Industries Shuttle, Mark 4, Heavy*.

Gods, she was almost wet with anticipation.

"Fairchild," Odille's voice had gone up half an octave. "Something strange is happening with that dust storm. Recommend you shear off and let this one go."

Yeah. Strange, all right. Even Riggel III hadn't been able to kick up a storm with this much power. Dani had never heard of any planet yet that could.

This was gonna be awesome.

"Still on the beam, Ground Station Beta," Dani replied coolly. "See you in two hours."

Never let them know she would have worked for free, just to have moments like this on strange, alien worlds.

It was getting intense. Choppy. Like riding an angry bull or a horny fireman.

Outside pressures would be popping her ears right now if she was out in that crap. The abrasives in the howling wind would leave fine scratches on anything softer than the two-centimeter-thick diamond windshield between her and the storm. Even the tough metal hull of her steed would probably be polished clean by this one.

Now the air was turning solid. The whitewater was hard and furious, coming for her soul.

The Shuttle's dull, gray, metal solidity actually bounced across air pockets too big for the blunt lifting surface on the little canards up front or the bigger deltas aft to control.

Dani dialed up the engine power and pushed the nose of her bull down, looking for the thicker air where the fun would really be found.

This was the kind of power that made her heart race. BASE jumping off space-scrapers could only barely approximate the run of speed before the human body hit terminal velocity.

Dani goosed the engines a little higher yet as the air fought her. Outside, the canards were starting to lift the nose, all by themselves, so she leaned her weight hard into the control yoke to hold the line as all that energy washed over her.

One quick glance to confirm that the scanners were transmitting everything cleanly back to base. Understanding a storm like this one would go a long ways towards deciphering the whole meteorological cycle for the planet.

And it gave her something to do.

"Fairchild," Odille called suddenly. "Abort, abort, abort. Eleven o'clock and closing hard. Get sky, girl!"

Dani sneered at the universe.

Dr. Chike was a boffin. Maybe he'd done commercial, industrial fishing on the homeworld to pay for college, but he'd grown soft into middle age.

Dani was never middle-aging.

"I did warn you, dearie," Eleanor sneered at her. But she did that anyway.

Nothing was too minor for Eleanor to complain about. Nothing.

Dani glanced at the radar feed from Beta's antenna as something beeped plaintively.

And then glanced again.

Oh, shit.

Was that even possible?

Radar was radar. You fired a loud, focused radio ping at the sky and listened for the reply. Time to echo indicated vector, the distance and direction.

Intensity indicated power.

Dust storms were an active force of nature, reshaping and sculpting planets. But this was something entirely else brewing.

The winds of a good storm started off generating creep as they pushed stuff across the ground, like water moving gravel. Once you had enough power, you got saltation as the sand and lighter stuff became airborne. The really light stuff, the dust or the fragments of larger bits that got smashed, ended up in suspension, flying like little bugs.

That was the dust cloud everyone watched on the evening news when it suddenly erupted, like a surprise pie in the face. Normally, they were about that dangerous, too, if you took care.

And saltation made it even more fun when it induced a static electricity field across the particles, a negative charge relative to the ground that caused more particles to be cast aloft and ground up. Every dust storm generated some level of static electricity. The Science Shuttle was specifically shielded, both internally and externally, to ignore the intense charge in the air.

Hell, she could fly right through a real thunderstorm, letting lightning strike the hull of the craft, and be perfectly safe. She'd done it, any number of times on Riggel III and other places.

This beast in front of her barely had any lightning, or moisture of any kind.

Sand storm.

So far, so good.

But that was a wall of solid, electrical charge coming at her. The radar thought it was a force field, maybe, or a permanent lightning bolt fifty kilometers across and twenty tall. And it was coming at her at a closing rate of over seven hundred kph, between the mad, avalanche rush down the mountainside and her own engines pushing forward.

Like riding an angry bull or a horny fireman.

Even the Shuttle thought she was about to fly into the side of a mountain now, regardless of the fact that there were none close and she was above them all anyway.

Various flight system warnings began to chirp madly.

Dani's lizardbrain wanted to jerk back on the yoke and slam the power to the stops to throw herself into the sky. It took everything she had not to react. That was the difference between dumb-kid Dani and oh-so-much-more-mature-and-calm Dani.

Never say middle-age. Old people were White Picket Fence.

She'd rather be dead than dreary.

Besides, as nasty as those winds were, that sort of response right now, trying to pull up and run for it, might cause her to turn turtle without even realizing it. At this altitude and speed, she'd hit the ground like one of those javelin probes from orbit before she even knew what happened.

There was only one way through this bitch storm right now anyway, threading the needle of her Shuttle through some class five and class six whitewater.

Dani took a tighter grip on the flight yoke as she glanced down at the airspeed indicator. It and the ground-speed radar were locked in a heated argument and trading insults electronically, but that could be forgiven in the face of a tidal wave of electrically-charged air coming at her at roughly one hundred sixty kph.

Maybe this hadn't been the best idea, after all?

Anything I do and I'm dead.

This is why they hired me. I'm better than the storm is.

Dani took an unconscious deep breath and flexed all her muscles rigid as that wall of bright red on her scanner charged closer.

At least Eleanor had the courtesy to stay quiet. Or maybe she understood that her own survival was rather tied up with Dani's at this point. Just like every other time. Distraction snark right now would probably be detrimental to everyone's health and well-being.

Boom.

The only way to describe the sound on the hull was like driving a metal sports car with a canvas, convertible roof through a sudden squall. The waterfall of rain pouring off the roof of an Italian villa, heard from the inside of the vehicle as the rumble of the falling water overtook the screaming of the antique, internal combustion engine as you drove hard, just moments before spinning the steering wheel around tight and jamming on the brakes fast enough to keep from slamming Rudy's prize antique motorcar into a brick wall as she'd fishtailed it across wet bricks.

Her brother had gotten over it. After all, there were no scratches on the paint or anything.

Around her, the Shuttle wobbled.

She was white-water rafting in the nastiest zones and bouncing off rocks and water that had the same amount of torque, even if it was nothing but air.

And then something behind her went *spang*.

Maybe *snap*.

Whatever.

The yoke turned unresponsive, sluggish.

Dead.

Panels on both sides of her started to flash bright red signals and scream like colicky nieces and nephews in the dead of night.

This was very much not good.

"...child, do you...?" came over the radio, along with a burst of static that was physically painful to experience.

Something shattered behind her with the sound of tearing metal.

And then silence.

Absolute, dead nothingness.

The really eerie kind.

You've-just-lost-all-power from a cascading-hydraulic-failure kind.

The only sound besides Dani's harsh breathing was wind screaming wildly across the outer hull and wing deltas as the engines fell silent, a dead horse rotting in the sun.

You could kill a *Qunsahr Industries Shuttle, Mark 4, Heavy*, theoretically. Dani had come close, on Riggel III, but the subsequent flight investigation had discovered maintenance corners cut by a lazy ground crew. She had still managed to glide the beast in soft enough that only one front landing foot had to be replaced.

Dani wasn't going to be that lucky, today. She was riding a corpse. That bull had just died of heart failure mid-buck.

Instead of panicking, Dani reached out and scooped up the Aide containing Eleanor and stuffed it into the customized pocket of her emergency flight suit, right between her breasts. Where Eleanor could listen to her heart rate and monitor other vitals when Dani was doing crazy things.

Like every other time.

At whatever altitude Dani had lost everything, the ground was coming up from below like an angry shark smelling an injured sea lion.

"A pilot in a normal flight suit with a parachute would be a dead man right now, you know," Dani announced as she checked buckles and straps. "Aren't you glad I got permission to wear my free-glider instead?"

Eleanor harrumphed from Dani's tiny cleavage with an amazing level of disdain for an electronic lifeform without lungs.

"A normal pilot wouldn't need a free-glider right now, dearie," Eleanor sneered with an icy disdain she must have learned from Chloe. "They would be watching the bow wave from a safe distance and elevation, drinking tea, and measuring sciency things, wouldn't they?"

...and boring as hell...

Dani checked her consoles, but the best she got right now were a few yellow lights, and one big, green, virtual button on her main console as the shuttle suggested strenuously that she eject.

And then something else popped and that console went black.

Dani smelled smoke.

She pulled down her face mask, locked it in place, and felt the life support system pressurize from internal oxygen.

Lizardbrain took over now.

Lots and lots of training was designed to make this process automatic. Dead-drunk, half-asleep, and still automatic.

Feet together. Left arm on lap. Head back, spine straight and relaxed.

Right hand reaches down.

Locate the lever by touch. Push down in a hard but firm

motion and lock it to reveal a side panel that opens aftwards with a snap.

Middle finger into the recess. Giving fate the bird, as her old instructor used to say.

Jab hard, listen for the sound of whistling air as the electro-chemical timer ignites.

Pull right hand onto your lap.

Take a breath.

Cross your arms over your chest, protecting the boobs with the elbows.

WHOOSH!!!

Acceleration straight up. Whatever straight up happened to be at the moment she and the dying shuttle parted ways.

Free flight.

Freefall.

Nine-point-nine meters-per-second squared acceleration as gravity got her greedy fingers on Dani's toes, like a squid wanting to feed.

One hundred sixty kilometers per hour wind in the face, a blow like a sledgehammer only barely subdued by Dani's flight suit. Air temperature readings at sixty-eight degrees Celsius.

Tumbling ass over teakettle as the Shuttle disappeared from sight, somewhere below and behind her.

Not good…

CHAPTER TWO

CHIKE

"FAIRCHILD, DO YOU COPY?"

Dr. Chike Odille was practically yelling into the microphone by now.

Her signal telemetry had gone from Four and One to Zero and Five in a heartbeat as that wall of electrically-charged particles had washed over the shuttle's bow.

Chike was glad he was alone in the radio hut at Ground Station Beta, so nobody could see as he wiped sweat from his face and took a deep breath, staring at the cream-colored microphone stick in one dark hand, turning from chocolate brown to ebony as he squeezed all the blood out of his right fist.

Chike muttered a curse and a prayer to Elegua under his breath as the gravity hit home. He reached out to change the radio channel from the one dedicated to the shuttle to the one for everyone on the planet or in near orbit.

"Calypso, this is Ground Station Beta, Dr. Chike Odille," he intoned sepulchrally. "I am declaring an emergency."

He counted to ten silently.

"Chike, this is Giles," the response from orbit sounded a

bit rushed and breathless. "What's happening?"

Dr. Giles Jones-Parker. Overall Mission Director on his seventeenth planetary survey. The grand old man of xeno-archaeology.

Chike couldn't imagine a bigger contrast between two old friends and colleagues.

Giles was a tall and rail-thin Anglo from the ancient land of Wales in the way-northwest of Europe, back on Earth. Chike had been born in Cameroon and studied in East Lansing, Michiga;, a squat, heavy-set man with eyes like expectant coals and skin like ninety-two percent dark chocolate.

If both were bald on top, at least Chike kept his sides shaved as well, instead of that stringy, almost-hippie look that Giles managed.

"Fairchild was flying a storm mission in the primary shuttle, Giles," Chike replied, aware that anyone with a radio, in orbit aboard Calypso, or on the planet at one of the ground stations, could be listening in right now. Many would be, in another few minutes. "Something went wrong."

There. Leave it at that. Do not speculate over an open channel.

It might be that nothing happened and she was just out of radio contact due to some unknown meteorological phenomenon.

Chike Odille didn't believe that for a moment.

He knew in his bones that there were problems. Xeno-archaeology missions were always dangerous places. Even if this was only his fifth, compared to Giles's seventeen, Chike still had a nose for it.

"A storm, Dr. Odille?" Giles asked. It sounded like the older scholar might have been asleep and was only now surfacing from a dream. "Do we have anyone on the ground who is expert in xeno-meteorology?"

"Yes, Giles," Chike agreed. "I'll be transmitting all of the data from the station and the shuttle to Calypso shortly. And I will also have Hadley Swain review everything and let me know what she thinks. You should also break out the secondary shuttle and prepare for the possibility of a Search and Rescue mission. That storm will be washing over us here in another fifteen minutes or so."

Chike took a deep, calming breath and pushed a button on a wall computer console. It happily trilled at the attention and began sending its telegraph signal into the sky as fast as the geo-stationary Calypso could absorb the data.

"Mother of God, Chike," Giles gasped. "What the hell is that? I've never seen a storm front like that."

"Neither have I, Dr. Jones-Parker," Chike kept the hectoring out of his voice. He realized that Giles was flighty when he got nervous. "We will learn a great deal when we have the leisure. However, right now, I cannot locate my shuttle, or the pilot, on any of my scans. She is not responding to the radio. Please initiate emergency procedures aboard Calypso. We may need an all-hands effort."

"Yes. I heartily agree," Giles replied.

In the background of the radio, Chike heard the emergency sirens begin to wind up as Calypso transformed from stodgy survey vessel into a rescue force.

Hopefully, he was simply over-reacting and would be the butt of crew jokes for years. Not that any of them would mind, in their hearts, a scientist over-reacting to protect the crew, instead of one complacent about a possible loss.

The alternative was that Fairchild was out there, somewhere, down on an unknown and potentially hostile world, populated by whatever life forms and things the Elder Race had left behind when they disappeared.

Chike carefully set the microphone down and let go, afraid he might crush even the rigid plastic in his grip.

CHAPTER THREE

FAIRCHILD

HEAT.

Even through the layers of insulation and life-support that comprised her free-glider, Dani felt the dry, angry heat of the storm, like ants trying to get inside and bite her. She could only imagine what it must be like on the ground.

And the wind was simply insane.

On Earth, Dani knew she would hit a terminal velocity of two hundred kph fairly quickly and then stay there until she spread her wings or slammed into the ground. Everything she had studied about Escudra VI had suggested a rough-enough symmetry of atmosphere with the mother planet.

But the wall of furious wind was tumbling her backwards at some ungodly speed as well.

First off, stop panicking.

Dani heard the gruff voice of her first free-flight instructor again, as they did that very first tandem sky-dive over Utah, back on Earth. Her a thirteen-year-old know-it-all and him a fifty-something ex-paratrooper that out-massed her by a factor of three and possibly out-snarked her by a factor of one half. Which was really saying something, compared to most of the people she'd ever met.

Stop panicking. This is just gravity doing its thing. Birds do this all day. So do silly-ass flying squirrels like you.

Dani couldn't help but giggle at that.

Humans had dreamed of flying since Icarus tried and Daedalus succeeded.

Da Vinci. Joseph-Michel and Jacques-Étienne Montgolfier. Orville and Wilbur Wright. Chuck Yeager.

Going into the sky and coming back safe.

A regular pilot in a pressurized suit would have to deploy a parachute right now and end up getting blasted sideways, out of control and tumbling, dragged by winds that hit like a drunk and jealous boyfriend who was always sorry afterwards.

They would probably black out from the torque generated.

Dani didn't have to settle.

Not that she had planned it that way, but she always wore her free-glider suit instead of a standard suit when she was flying. It was already tailored for her slim figure, so it saved on expedition costs, money that could be sunk into better toys for the boffins.

Now, it was going to save her life.

Hopefully.

Skin-tight and navy blue in a flat, matte finish that wouldn't distract others nearby doing the same, crazy flying stunts. Wrapped tight around a body that some people compared to a twelve-year-old boy.

Of course, those were usually girls whose fashion sizes were steadily creeping up towards double-digits.

Meow.

Onboard life support for a couple of weeks here and

enough padding to keep her from bruising too badly on a rough landing.

Rigid helmet strapped tight. Blond hair cut short enough to stay inside and let it seal. Transparent semi-steel face plate with voice-activated Heads-Up-Displays that had everything from barometrics and flight sensors to the latest dance club videos, depending on need and attention span.

It was the gaps between limbs that made a free-glider fun. She really was a flying squirrel.

Soft fabric membranes with semi-rigid ribs connected wrist to ankle on both sides, with a lesser flap between her legs to help her stabilize when falling. Aileron-like flaps on her heels helped her steer and only deployed when there was enough windstream over them to overcome the springs that normally held them close against her body.

Free-gliding.

Take an aircraft up to around thirty thousand meters and bail out, along with a dozen of your closest enemies and the flavor of the month boyfriend. Contests for fastest to ground, longest glide time, greatest distance covered, or races to capture a flag, either on the ground or hanging from a tower or bridge.

Attack of the rabid, flying squirrels. Frequently while at least partly drunk.

Hopefully, all that juvenile stupidity would keep her alive now.

Step one, feet together and toes pointed. Lean back into the windstream.

Nobody ever understood that part.

Let Mercury's little ankle-bootie wings grab the airstream and turn you over, head pointed down like a javelin. It was too easy to lose track of the horizon and gravity, especially when you were doing this at night.

Make Newton do all the work for you.

Face down now, decide if you want to turn into the wind and stall, or run down it like a ski jumper getting ready for serious air.

The dust storm made everything a hazy pink. Visibility would be measured in decameters, not kilometers.

Dani decided to run with the storm for a while and let it bleed energy off before she tried to land and take stock.

She knew she had been north of Ground Station Beta by about seventy kilometers when everything went sideways, but right now, her compass was literally spinning counter-clockwise from the electromagnetism in the dust storm and the radio was a hash of newspapers being crumpled and torn apart.

Apparently, Escudra VI was a much more interesting place than she had been led to believe by the briefing packets.

Middle-age could wait a while.

Force hands and feet apart, head back, and let the force of her falling through atmosphere be converted to forward momentum. The dust storm would be running downhill. As long as she ran before it, she should be going away from the mountains.

Assuming she hadn't gotten on the far side of the macroburst and was going deeper into the range instead of closer to home.

Sun right now would be helpful. Flying blind in the gloaming was fine when you were a kid and winning a bet. Right now, it was her ass on the line.

At least Eleanor was quiet.

Although, considering the amount of electricity in the air, hopefully she wasn't dead.

Having nobody to talk to until the S&R teams showed up would probably drive Dani mad.

Deep breaths.

Oxygenize everything and let it burn out the adrenaline

threatening to make you sound like a rabid squirrel if you talked.

Radio: painful.

Compass: swirling and useless until she got out of the charge field of whatever she had flown into. Hopefully.

Altimeter: laughing madly and doing strange things as it crept down towards what it thought was zero. Or ground. Or splatter.

Visibility: dust.

Air Temperature: medium rare.

Airspeed Indicator: Okay, that was looking promising.

Dani couldn't remember ever hitting that speed on Earth, or anywhere else, but she'd also never tried doing something this amazingly dangerous before, either.

Still, record it and remember to send it off to the lovely folks in Ireland so she could get into their pretty, little book and thereafter could win bar bets and free drinks forever.

Dani tilted her head back more and curled her fists forward a scooche. Not much, at this speed, you didn't need much. Just enough to generate a little lift. Or rather, convert some of that mad forward momentum into lift, like an owl with a rabbit in its feet.

The airspeed indicator dropped back down from a probable galactic record to only completely insane as the altimeter decided that maybe she was flat enough and the ground wasn't about to bite her.

"System: comm off," Dani called over the harsh static in her ears.

Okay, maybe still a little too loud. Too much rabid and not enough squirrel in her voice.

Still, the radio stopped grinding gravel in her ears, leaving only the screaming whistle of the outside air channeling nooks and edges into sound.

Dani risked a glance back over a shoulder out of the

corner of her face plate. Maybe it was lighter over there. That might be the back side of the storm.

Maybe it was even starting to die out and she would be able to find ground soon.

Hopefully before it found her.

Better to sneak up on the thing. It was like morning sobriety, that way. Best found by accident and quickly rectified.

I can turn into it and maybe get blasted ass over tea kettle again. Or I can do it the crazy way.

Dani smiled.

Like that was even an option where she was concerned.

She leaned back hard and pushed her legs together while spreading her arms like angel wings.

Aerial gymnasts on the ground only wished they could do this. They might have more control, but they still had to land afterwards.

Dani turned a perfect back pike, tucked into a cannonball at the top of the fall, and rolled onto her left side before splaying her arms out wide suddenly, like flashing her naked chest at a stranger from a third story window.

Or something to that effect.

Now she was falling into the wind, gliding like a big, blue eagle on bucking thermals as the outflow boundary got further and further away from her heels.

The air was darker here, but that was her getting lower, rather than the nasty shit getting thicker.

Nothing but eerie darkness below.

It was almost like scuba diving after a storm.

Not like the Terran Caribbean, where the water would be clear and the sand white.

No, murky. Maybe on the northeast parts of the Pacific Ocean, or Hyanduse Reef back home on Panamuer Nuevo.

Like sharks might swim out of the dust suddenly and

sniff her for food sign. Or a killer whale might start to blow a bubble net around her with ten of his closest, hungry friends.

Still, the madness of the storm had receded some. Blown past her in its rage and hunger to go chase someone else.

"System: headlights on," Dani said, much more evenly, possibly even reverentially, although she would never admit it. The shadows and gloom reminded her of an ancient, almost-forgotten church she had once visited in Jalisco. The quiet as well.

Two bright lights lanced out of her skull, like ram's horns.

At least nothing loomed from the dark suddenly. No sharks or angry whales. No dragons rising up as she turned her head right and left to cut through the dust.

The wind was dying as well.

Or maybe she was coming down off the high. It was hard to tell.

Dani settled for a scallop now.

Tilt forward in a pike to gain speed and drop elevation, then pull back almost enough to stall.

Repeat, going down like curved steps on a staircase.

Took forever, but it was still the safest way to get to ground in the dark, as long as you didn't fly into a mountain, or a building, or a car.

Around her, the air temperature was dropping as well. Down from frying eggs on hoods to soft-boiling them, but still.

She could feel the sigh of relief as her internal cooling system against her shoulder blades had a chance to back off the compressor some. The sound of fans and pumps went down slightly as well, adding to the eerie silence.

More scallops, more stair steps. Slow, methodical, safe.

Never say boring. Sounds too much like middle-age. Or worse, grown-up.

Grrrrrr.

Something loomed, breaking Dani out of her monotony.

She squinted as the shape emerged from the fog and dust.

Oh, shit.

MOUNTAIN.

Her lights revealed whole crags as ground suddenly became a thing.

Dani leaned back and threw herself to her left as hard as she could as a cliff-face appeared out of nowhere.

She almost made it, too.

Another meter, perhaps half that, and she could have squeezed past, or maybe stalled sharp enough to grab on and pretend to free-climb the steep hillside.

Instead, Dani heard her helmet clunk solidly against rock, and the squid that was gravity got hold of her toes.

She start tumbling backwards down a small avalanche of scree.

And then darkness.

CHAPTER FOUR

CHIKE

CHIKE STOPPED in the open door to the comm room and reached out his left hand to locate the emergency button that would rouse the entire camp. He took a moment to look around the rest of the small quad that made up Ground Station Beta, at least as much of it as they had managed to unpack and set up after landing in the over-sized meadow on this upland plateau.

It had been quiet, up until now.

It was about to get crazy.

The kitchen hut: a dark green, semi-soft deployable building, like an old-fashioned canvas tent that magically turned to rigid walls when you applied the right current for three seconds. Filled with microwaves, refrigerators, water, and a portable coffin freezer to keep the crew happy and fat.

Radio hut: an archaic, apparently military term dating back to the dawn of the stellar age, when one man or woman had a coffin-sized radio made from finger-sized vacuum-tubes to talk to others with, instead of a portable server farm with a semi-intelligent AI, really just a smart system, to handle all the data and communication tasks.

Break hut: four stalls of showers and two walls of absurdly high-tech incinerating toilets. The crew would happily sleep rough for weeks, as long as they could get a warm shower occasionally and didn't have to squat in the weeds with the local analog of rattlesnakes.

Convention center: conference room, planning table, visual comm screens, karaoke machine. Right now, half the ground crew were hot-bunking in there, while the others were in two-person popup shelters, scattered around the ring of central buildings like an outbreak of hives, or a convention of giant gophers.

Ten minutes ago, before Fairchild had disappeared, it had been just another planetary survey mission. Several big-name planetologists on grants, a few professional support staff, and three gaggles of undergrad and post-grad students on an adventure or a professional expedition. Or both. Certainly beat the hell out of digging for Bronze Age artifacts in central England, save for the lack of a good corner pub to bip down to for a pint.

Maybe they would need to include that in the next grant proposal. A stellar publican could have a field day out here, with a captive audience. Maybe custom-build an inflatable shelter like the rest, and figure out how to have a bar that turned into a wood veneer with enough current applied.

Chike smiled. And then remembered where he was. What he was supposed to be doing.

The Emergency.

His left hand opened the cover over the switch.

Deep breath.

We have a problem.

He pressed the big, red switch underneath, letting go to cover his ears as the air raid siren woke the dead and frightened any native critters within a kilometer.

Heads popped up out of tents and from doorways almost

immediately, many scrambling in his direction half-dressed and pulling on pants, shirt, or shoes. Hadley Swain, the post-grad in xeno-meteorology he probably needed the most right now, didn't even bother with that, sprinting from the showers still covered in soap.

Chike counted to eight and punched the switch to kill the alarm. No reason to make everyone's head ring.

He looked around at the expectant faces as the camp gathered, until he found the face he wanted.

Ann-Marta Thorgisdaughter. Ground Services Coordinator, Security, Search and Rescue Commander.

Den Mother.

Both sides of her family had left places in East Africa during the Twentieth Century Diaspora and ended up in Sweden. Her body was slim and her skin was chocolate milk to his asphalt, and there was nobody better equipped for the job.

"We have lost contact with Fairchild," Chike announced, loud enough that everyone in the camp would hear.

Best to get it out early and not beat around the bush.

Don't overplay. Don't minimalize.

"She was flying a storm mission and some sort of massive electrical disturbance came up," he continued as voices alternately gasped and murmured. Everyone liked Fairchild, as near as he could tell. "Her signal has disappeared from the comm and the radar, but we're entirely blind and can't see into the heart of that storm right now."

Everything came to stillness as the gravity of the situation took hold.

"I have notified Dr. Jones-Parker and declared a formal emergency," Chike declared. "Calypso is breaking out the other shuttle. Ann-Marta will be in charge of operations from this point forward."

She nodded at him from across the space and indicated that he should keep speaking.

"Search and Rescue teams should shift to field operations planning," Chike continued.

Usually, that was for when someone had wandered into a box canyon and gotten turned around and silent without a clear line to the right navigational satellite. This was a little more serious.

"Atmosphere teams, drop what you were doing and start processing the data we have from the storm so we can create search patterns and figure out how much risk there is to the camp when that storm front gets here in another fifteen minutes. Move it people."

And just like that, the mob scattered as rapidly as it had assembled. Asses and elbows going every which way, including a nice one on Hadley Swain as she raced back to finish her shower.

Chike found Ann-Marta as his elbow.

"How bad is the storm?" she asked quietly.

She did everything quietly, even when she had to impose herself on drunk and rowdy undergrads.

Chike took a moment to consider his response.

"I've never seen a dust storm generate that much electromagnetic disturbance, even in labs," he said. "The shuttle should be tough enough to handle it, but we should have heard something by now."

"Could Fairchild be surfing the winds inside the storm, flying in circles where she can't talk to us?" Ann-Marta probed.

Oh, yes. She knew Fairchild's reputation for competence tinged with crazy.

"Right now, A.M.," Chike said, "I would be happy to be labeled the fussy, old hen who over-reacts."

"And?"

"And I've got a bad feeling."

Ann-Marta studied his face for several moments, looking for something. She was almost as tall as he was, and perhaps half his mass, but she was a warrior and he was an academic. A slightly-pudgy, middle-aged field researcher.

Chike could see Vikings in her cultural ancestry, and probably her bloodlines somewhere as well.

"Okay," she decided. "How bad is the storm? And how big?"

"Dunno," Chike replied. "The wall is huge and wide. It has slowed down from that first mad rush as the tower collapsed, but it will still roll right over us like a sand storm in a few minutes. And we can't see through it."

"You said an electromagnetic signature as well?" she continued.

"That's right. Big enough that we might get static electricity off metal surfaces. The servers should be insulated, but I want to shut down all non-essentials, just in case."

"Good idea," Ann-Marta agreed. "And get everyone out of the huts. They can shelter in tents, but the buildings might revert if the induced current is enough."

That shook him. Those huts were supposed to be proof against lightning strikes, being well-insulated themselves and carefully grounded. But this was a rolling lightning bolt, racing across the ground at them like a gaseous electric eel, looking for a soft belly to bite into.

Chike wondered if his rugged field camera would be able to capture video of it. Equipment guarantees were one thing. He wanted evidence if the impossible actually happened.

Escudra VI was turning out to be much more interesting than anyone had anticipated. Hopefully, that would make his career better, too.

But first, Fairchild.

He couldn't imagine someone less likely to need anyone

else's assistance, but this planet was trying to prove him wrong on everything else.

Ann-Marta nodded.

"I'm sure she's fine," the Viking woman declared.

Chike wished he could agree.

CHAPTER FIVE

FAIRCHILD

"I KNOW you're not dead, Danielle," the angry, hectoring voice intruded on her darkness, forcing her to bob to the surface from an especially dark and quiet place. Sleep had been nice. "It would be helpful if you would get off me and let me look around."

Eleanor.

That was Eleanor's voice. Muffled and tinged with a bit of nervous energy, but certainly her Governess.

Dani decided she must have had one hell of a good time last night. She hadn't had a hangover like this in years. Everything hurt, not just her head.

And damn, this bed was hard.

Dani considered rolling over and going back to sleep. Eleanor could wait until the sun came up, at the very least.

"And I would appreciate an explanation of how we came to be here, young lady," Eleanor ranted on. "And whatever it was you did to my short-term memory files. I've lost more than an hour of realtime."

How would Eleanor lose an hour of realtime? That would require…

Dani sat bolt upright with a gasp of intense pain. Her whole right side hurt, crown to ankle, like the time she had slipped and fallen backwards off the speaker stack at that one concert where she had been go-go dancing topless.

"Ow," she groaned, seeing cute little stars and waterbugs racing around her head in the dim sky.

At least everything was still attached. And not spinning too badly.

The twin headlights were still on, cutting a path into the dusty darkness around her. The suit was feeding her air from the recycling plant.

Dani found herself slightly buried, about half a body deep, in pea-sized gravel that looked vaguely pink in the white light. She wiggled her butt until the rocks settled under her instead of against her and over her legs.

Standing up might be a bit much to ask right now.

Right arm hurt, but moved normally and hung at the right angle. Probably not broken. Ditto the leg.

Dani took a moment to unhook all her flight membranes and dump out all the gravel they had accumulated so everything would retract tight against her skin.

"System: comm on," she said.

No response.

"System: comm unit activate," Dani repeated, louder.

Still nothing.

"Let me look at you, Dani," Eleanor said in a much more quiet and concerned voice.

Dani figured that would help. She pulled the Aide from her breast pocket and held it up at arm's length so the Governess could scan her.

"Well, that explains part of it," Eleanor announced in a voice somewhere between smug and fearful.

"What?" Dani asked, her brain only slightly back on line at this point.

"You hit your head on something sharp," Eleanor replied. "Hard enough to penetrate the helmet's outer casing. How's your air?"

Dani sucked in a quick breath. Nothing special.

Onboard air. Headlights. Gravel.

She had been free-gliding in a dust storm after bailing out of a dead shuttle.

Darkness. Electrical interference. MOUNTAIN.

Her life support system still held. Apparently only the electronic computer had gotten a concussion. Or a worse one. Her organic one was doing pretty well, considering.

"Life support seems fine," Dani said aloud. "System: lights off."

Nothing.

Dani realized that the Heads-Up-Display she was used to living with wasn't there. Nothing but clear steel between her and the planet.

She reached up her right hand and found the spot where her skull had kissed the mountain, just above her right temple. Sure enough, she could poke a finger through the outer layer of a material that was supposed to be bullet-proof.

At least the inner layer had held.

And the helmet's external controls were ambidextrous.

Dani reached up with her left hand, the one that didn't hurt nearly as much, and flipped the radio button manually.

Nothing.

She must have really smashed it good.

For a moment, Dani nearly panicked.

Being lost was one thing. It was, in fact, a total adventure on the right planet, like Escudra VI might be.

But that presupposed a working radio, so she could call for help if things got out of hand.

Like now.

The electronic compass was as dead as the System was, if she couldn't turn it on.

"Eleanor," Dani said. "We might have a problem."

"Oh, dear," Eleanor scoffed. "You noticed? I was hoping to keep it a secret."

"Not helping, Eleanor."

"Well excuse me for computating, young lady," the Aide snarked back savagely, her voice rising and growing louder. "Last I knew, we were about to fly into a thunderstorm instead of around it like I had first suggested. Now the Shuttle's gone, you're hurt, and we're lost on this stupid planet, and…"

"Control Override," Dani barked. "Null emotion reset."

Eleanor dropped instantly to silence.

The silence felt wonderful, at least for a little bit. Too much silence and Dani might find herself gnawing on the walls.

It happened, occasionally.

"Thank you," Eleanor whispered in a much calmer, flatter voice. "What happened?"

"No prob," Dani replied. "It's messy."

She shook her head a little harder and nothing rattled loose. Pain level about a three on a ten point scale.

Briefly, she considered standing up, but thought better of it when she realized that the slope of the mountain she was sitting on kept going down for a long ways. Not cliff-face, but one pitch and she'd ass-over-teakettle for a kilometer pretty easily.

The sky was full night, lit by stars, three small moons in various phases, and the twin beams from her ram's skull.

"Shuttle died mid-flight," Dani continued, aiming the lights down-slope to survey her terrain options. "We were flying into and through the hot parts of the dust storm's outflow boundary. That was fine. Then something failed."

"Failed?"

Eleanor's voice sounded almost robotic, but that was the factory-reset. Even AI's could panic. It was useful to be able to hit them with the electronic equivalent of a double shot of whiskey.

She'd be good as new in a few minutes.

"Hydraulic system ruptured somewhere," Dani replied. "That would have been okay, but whatever happened took out the rest of the electronics and I was flying a falling brick at four thousand meters ground elevation."

"I see."

"Grabbed you. Bailed into the sky. Rode the free-glider down and out into the dust storm."

Dani stretched her legs. Everything felt okay, more or less.

She decided to try standing.

Pull the legs underneath. Yeah, that worked.

Lean forward and put hands down. Whoa. Maybe a touch slower. Head's still a little iffy.

Squat and drive *slowly* vertical. Only wobble a little.

Victory.

Now don't fall down a mountain, ya big goof.

"As we were gliding, we found a mountain. Or something."

"Where are we?" Eleanor asked in a careful, almost fearful voice.

Her tone was getting better. Quieter, but there were emotional traces sneaking in. Fear and despondency, but that was better than nothing.

Right?

"Dunno," Dani shrugged, and immediately regretted it as all the nerves on her right side lit up like fire. "Mmmmph."

She sucked a hard breath down to her toes and let it wash all the bad mojo away, like turning a firehose on the kids at a party to get them to take their action somewhere else.

Or words to that effect. Dani would never do anything so uncouth.

Sober, that is.

"Was free-gliding for fifteen, maybe twenty minutes," Dani continued. "Don't know with the electronics zarked. I don't even know where north is, at least until the sun comes up."

"I see," Eleanor responded flatly.

Dani wasn't sure a panicky, snarky, semi-abusive Governess wouldn't be an improvement over this flat, semi-void of a person. At least Eleanor was programmed to not hate Dani after the few times she had to trigger the mode over the years.

It was like dealing with Tina, one of the times when she had mixed the wrong brain pills with too much booze and went total zombie for four hours. But Tina and Eleanor would both kind of agree with any proposition when that happened.

Dani didn't need artificial stimulants to agree, most of the time.

"So what happened to my memory?" Eleanor asked.

There was definitely an edge there now, if a little ragged. Fear. Hurt. Possible betrayal.

Nobody liked waking up with no memory of the last few hours, in a strange place, frequently with total strangers and sometimes with a lack of clothes.

At least nobody had put anything in her drinks, this time.

Still…

"The dust storm triggered some sort of tertiary, electromagnetic effect," Dani said. "Shuttle's scanners and radar saw it as a solid wall, so I can only imagine what the signature looked like. Hopefully Chike Odille and the gang at Beta got a good sniff of it before we lost the transmitter. We were partly through it and starting to head out the back when the ship failed, but I had to pretty much abandon ship right into the nastiest parts of it. Wouldn't surprise me if it scrambled your RAM pretty good. How's your ROM doing?"

RAM. Random Access Memory. Short term stuff. The last few minutes of whatever was going on, whatever comm number you needed to remember. The cute girl's name. Little stuff.

As opposed to ROM. Read Only Memory. *Important Files* put in a box and locked. Stored in the attic against need.

Memories.

"Scanning," Eleanor replied.

Dani let the silence pass.

The slope below her was maybe one in six now. Six meters forward, one meter down. A haul, but nothing compared to what was above her as she turned around and looked. That looked like one in two, or maybe two in one.

It got vertical up there in places.

Dani wondered where she had hit, and how far she had fallen.

She was standing in a small puddle of gravel, and had apparently carried it with her in a micro-avalanche from someplace farther up the slope.

Somewhere, up there, there was a rock with a head-print on it.

Dani flipped the entire mountain off with both hands, a silent salute to surviving.

"Was that really necessary, dear?" Eleanor asked.

The snark was back. Hopefully, Eleanor was back as well.

"Nope," Dani replied with a savage, survivor's grin. "Felt good."

"Fine," Eleanor retorted. "But next time, could you put

me in your pocket first? I get a little motion sick from sudden gestures of juvenile aggression."

Dani actually felt her cheeks redden, inside the helmet where, hopefully, Eleanor couldn't see.

"Sorry," Dani mumbled, putting her hands down by her sides, before lifting her hand back up so she could see Eleanor's face on the little display.

Eleanor had been programmed with a diamond-shaped face. Prominent cheekbones dominated a long face with a high forehead and a small chin. It was a face of a Governess: intellectual, beautiful, and tough.

"All systems green?" Dani asked.

"At present, yes. What's next?"

Good question.

Dani turned back to the valley below her, so she and Eleanor could see.

Escudra VI's moons were all tiny rocks locked in temporary, millennia-long orbits instead of a big one like Earth had. Nothing that would have generated decent tides. Not like Luna.

When it got dark at night, it was like a new moon on Earth. Ten billion stars visible from this location in the local arm, but the mountains around her had to be deduced from the deeper darkness they cast.

Still, it was local summer, more or less, in this hemisphere. Escudra VI had only a minor axial tilt, so the seasonal variance would be minimal. The storm had left things warmer than normal, but Dani wasn't about to pop her lid off to sniff the place if she didn't have to.

The life support in her suit would keep things regulated, even mechanically, for a week or more, provided she didn't do anything stupid or damage it any more than she had.

Dani opened her mouth wide enough to pop her jaw and yawn.

Down had settled into down finally and her head was only ringing a little bit.

Not like any of the times she had managed a concussion. She could hear, even. That was always a good sign.

Around her, fields of gravel.

No plants, trees, or itinerant fauna looking back.

The dust was a fine haze now, rather than a morning fog casting a pall over everything. Headlight visibility was probably two hundred meters now if she held her head still.

Dani found herself standing on something of a mountain saddle.

Big, ugly mountain behind her fell away in all directions, but right here it kind of flattened out into a thing that could be charitably called a highland meadow, if there had been any clover or grass growing up here.

Not that Escudra VI had much, and the treeline was supposedly receding every century as water either evaporated out into space, or got pulled down into the rocks and bound into oxides and nitrates.

"How far can you scan?" Dani asked Eleanor with a serious tone for once.

She watched Eleanor screw up her face in concentration on the little screen and squint.

Recently, Eleanor had taken on an avatar with semi-long brown hair that she usually wore up in a bonnet or hat in a style she had explained as Victorian.

Something pre-space flight. Antique. Like Rudy's vintage ground cars with internal combustion engines.

Today she was wearing a tight bodice in a brownish-maroon over what looked like a cream-colored silk blouse, with a very high collar.

Dani would feel strangled in that kind of outfit, but she supposed that an artificial lifeform AI could present herself however she felt, since she could never get an outfit dirty.

It was not like Dani followed that many fashion rules, herself, most of the time.

Generally inversely proportional to the expectations of the situation, if just to drive her family nuts. She knew she looked good. She didn't have to dress like a show pony to prove it.

"Something's off, somewhere," Eleanor finally responded. "My scanning range is strangely curtailed. Possibly as a result of the storm and electrical phenomena."

"So we'd have to be close enough to pee on them, if I was a boy?" Dani asked with a grin.

"Perhaps a bit more than that, dear," Eleanor tartly observed. "Even with a tail wind."

A pause.

"And my radio functions are not picking up the navigation satellites I would normally use to triangulate with. I'm sure, again, all your fault."

At least Eleanor projected a smile when she said that. Dani was beginning to wonder if maybe she had finally managed to get the two of them into something over her head.

Not for lack of trying for the better part of two decades. But this might be more than she could talk her way out of or around.

That was an exceptionally unpleasant place to dwell.

"Well, I would like to sleep some," Dani announced, risking a few steps onto what looked like it might be more stable ground. Or at least less gravel. "Hopefully nothing can sneak up on you. I'm bushed and not thinking straight."

"I will guard you like a lioness, Danielle," Eleanor said.

That just made it worse.

Eleanor only called her by her given name when Dani was in a lot of trouble, or really, really depressed.

Dani let her butt find stone and stretched herself out until she found a piece of ground that was flat enough that she didn't hurt too badly.

She was asleep in moments.

CHAPTER SIX

CHIKE

ALL THE BIG huts were empty.

Everyone was waiting inside one of the small tents, theoretically insulated, grounded, and safe from what was about to happen outside the carefully-sealed-up mini-shelters.

Chike was taking bets with himself.

Somehow, he had ended up in a two-person tent with Ann-Marta and Hadley Swain, who was at least now clean, mostly dry, and even dressed, if a damp T-shirt and baggy expedition pants counted.

Chike knew he should pay less attention, but her lovely smell was distracting in the confined quarters.

And he was far too old for her.

He gave up and turned to face Ann-Marta, who had a knowing grin on her face and a portable sensor slab in her hands.

Chike felt his skin grow an increment darker with blush.

At least anybody but Ann-Marta wouldn't probably be able to discern it. Not in this light, anyway.

He settled for gripping his own slab more tightly and

running through the diagnostics on the screen. Every camera, sensor, or weather pack the team could get out and up in six minutes was deployed somewhere within twenty meters of him, furiously recording every bleat and hiccup as they all waited with baited breath.

"Chike," Hadley said to get his attention, leaning too close and pointing at a readout on his screen. "Are we sure that the calibrations are correct? That says sixty-two degrees Celsius outside and rising. Is that even possible?"

Chike turned to grin at her without otherwise moving.

"I remember a story I heard from a xeno-meteorologist about a storm in Texas, on Earth, in the very early days of the space age."

"Kopperl, Texas," she replied with a sudden nod. "*Satan's Storm*. I had forgotten. But that temperature spike peaked out at sixty degrees Celsius and even that quickly faded. And the clocked winds only reached one hundred twenty kph for a very brief time before they faded as well. What makes you certain this storm will be so much more dangerous?"

Chike had to remember that underneath that brown-eyed, bottle-blond, pretty face was a brain like a computer and a talent that would probably have her commanding her own expeditions soon. Pretty girls weren't supposed to be that smart, and smart ones weren't supposed to be that pretty.

It was like they were violating one of the laws of thermodynamics.

"Because there were temperature readings from Fairchild at close to seventy Celsius, clear up at her altitude, Hadley," Chike said with a serious mien. This was a pair of scientists discussing theories and findings, not a too-pretty girl close enough to befuddle his higher brain functions. "Also, the sustained winds at that point were one hundred sixty kph. If you collapse the storm head atop that, and run the entire boundary downhill, which we have done, it's likely to have maintained, if not accelerated as it crossed the intervening terrain. It happens."

"You've been through something like this before," she accused sharply.

Chike glanced at Ann-Marta, who nodded solemnly back at him at the memory of Riggel III.

He turned back to Hadley.

"Possibly worse," he hazarded a guess. "But that was just a thunderstorm with rain and hailstones the size of fists. This will be a sirocco with a lightning genie bottled up and being drug along kicking and screaming behind, much like my four-year-old nephew used to do."

Hadley leaned back and her eyes flared a little wider.

Brilliant academic, but she was on her first serious dig as a post-grad working towards her doctorate. Things out here this afternoon were far more serious than drinking, dancing, and partying. Or, in Hadley's case, reading constantly in a quiet corner of some tent.

Lives were possibly on the line, and her expert background in xeno-meteorology put her in the command tent where those decisions would be made.

Chike watched the young woman suddenly change gears. It was like seeing her turn into a grown-up before his eyes, or maybe that same transformation that always came over Ann-Marta when things got tight.

Good. She understood.

Without a word, Hadley looked down and consulted her own slab, furious typing and swiping across the screen for several seconds.

"We will see seventy-six degrees sustained for at least sixty seconds, with a surge peak of seventy-eight," she said in a tight voice. "Winds will sustain at one hundred forty kph, with gusts to one hundred fifty-five. Dr. Odille, do you agree?"

"You are within three percent of my guestimates, experience, and calculations, Hadley."

She paled, just a little, and reached out, almost unconsciously, to touch the side of the tent. Already, the winds outside were audible.

At least the tent was rigid enough to protect them for now, assuming that an induced current didn't cause the shell to collapse back into fabric.

And it wouldn't tear, not without something moving faster than this wind.

Ann-Marta's first rule of planetfall was to set the anchor spikes deep and solid before the tents and buildings deployed.

Even Chike wasn't in charge of his own Base Camp until the Ground Services Coordinator was satisfied.

Where they sat would hold.

But he could only imagine what Fairchild must be going through as the winds suddenly surged around them. He thought he heard the walls creak with the strain.

He glanced back at Ann-Marta and they shared a common memory of that hell-storm on Riggel III. Fairchild had missed that one, safely in orbit aboard Zheng He.

Even a sturdy craft like a survey shuttle would have suffered damage from some of the ice balls that had fallen from the sky. Chike really didn't believe a lump of ice the size of a football qualified as *hail*.

"Mary, Mother of God," Hadley whispered, staring at the screen in front of her. "Can Fairchild survive this?"

Chike nodded and shared another semi-secret grin with Ann-Marta.

"If something happened to the shuttle, she can always bail out," Ann-Marta replied. "She's in a special, custom flight suit designed for hostile environments and vacuum. I'm more worried that the storm will mess up all of our electronics and we won't be able to find her quickly."

"I see," Hadley said quietly, eyes and mind still focused on her readouts. She looked up suddenly at Chike with a gleam in her eyes like an eagle spotting a salmon trying to sneak upstream.

"I call dibs on Escudra VI electrical mega-storms as a dissertation topic," she announced quietly.

Chike chuckled and grinned at her.

"That, young lady, is between you and your faculty advisor when you get home," he said. "You are, however, the only xeno-meteorologist on site and will therefore be the galactic subject matter expert in a few hours."

"I've read some about Riggel III, Dr. Odille," Hadley said. "That was just Earth weather on a grander scale, correct?"

"Correct," he agreed. "This will apparently be something bigger. Hopefully, reasonably rare, because our automated probes either did not record an event like this, or if they had, it was discounted as faulty equipment."

Around them, the walls started to vibrate with energy.

Chike glanced down at the little regulator box in the corner, striving mightily to blow cool air into the room as the heat outside approached the level where efficiency broke down.

"Countdown to impact," Hadley announced. "Or whatever you want to call the intersection of that wall of electromagnetism with our position. We are seeing the speed begin to fade with distance from the center, elapsed time, and ground friction. Outside speeds are sustaining at one hundred ten kph, but the temperatures are still above seventy Celsius. Ten seconds to storm front."

Chike hoped that she had remembered to broadcast that

to all the other tents. He had the only weather expert handy in here with him. Most of the rest were planetology specialists, experts in the ground, not the sky. Fairchild was probably the next best sky adept handy.

The entire tent felt like it wanted to take off, one solid wall actually leaning just the slightest bit as the winds got louder outside.

"And, contact," Hadley yelled as the wall image on her screen moved across the camp.

Everything *changed* in an instant.

It couldn't penetrate the insulated and grounded walls, but the air itself felt like it polarized. Or maybe the polarization flipped.

He felt Ann-Marta's hand on his shoulder, providing the kinds of strength the chocolate Viking was known for.

Hadley kind of shrank in on herself at the rampant sound and fury, so Chike put his hand on her shoulder.

Human contact, in the face of nature's grand fury. As if Ann-Marta's strength could flow through him and into the other woman.

It might.

Moments passed. Or minutes. It was hard to measure.

"All sensor packs have now overloaded and reset, or rebooted entirely," Hadley said. "Next time, we'll need to build tougher gear. Might have to have a talk with some of Calypso's electrical engineers. I have some ideas."

Chike nodded. He did as well. This storm, this planet, was likely to make the careers of a number of the people here in Beta today.

He was already well-known, but Chike was a planetologist. A xeno-geologist/vulcanist. The underground signals he would be pursuing were already fascinating and hinted at big and deep secrets to be uncovered. If Hadley Swain played her cards right, she might be an Expedition

Lead next time he worked with her, and he might be on her team, instead of the other way around.

It would make a nice symmetry.

Chike pushed a physical button on his slab and waited while a little wheel icon spun as the radio systems tried to punch through the mass of static overhead.

The signal locked in, but the icon flashed yellow angrily with the number 2/3 presented. Barely adequate contact to talk to Calypso, even with the transmission boosters available at both ends. Lots of squelch.

"Calypso, this is Ground Station Beta, do you read?" Chike enunciated clearly.

"Affirmative, Chike," the ghost of a voice came back through a nearly-painful amount of static. It sounded like Giles. "What is your status?"

"Hopefully, the worst is over, Giles," Chike said a little louder. "We are still waiting for the winds to die down some before we emerge to take stock. What do you see from orbit, Calypso?"

"I don't know weather all that well, Dr. Odille," Giles replied. "From what I can see, the storm is rapidly breaking up. If you had been fifteen or twenty kilometers farther from the epicenter, you might not have gotten nearly as heavy an impact. At thirty kilometers, you might not have noticed. Has Ms. Swain had a chance to study everything?"

"I'm here, Dr. Jones-Parker," Hadley spoke up. "We have deployed our full package and turned it to verbose logging for this."

"Excellent, Hadley," Giles voice contained all the excitement of a six-year-old on Christmas morning, even through the static. "We'll be counting on you to take point on this one. And probably headline the study we'll need to publish when we get home."

Chike had to bite his tongue not to laugh out loud at the

look of pure glee that came over the young scientist's face. Ann-Marta squeezed his deltoid muscle almost enough to hurt to keep him from making any response.

Yes, that would make Hadley Swain a household name in the small field of galactic studies.

Now they just had to go find Fairchild, once everything calmed down to the point that nobody else would be at risk, trying to get to wherever she was.

CHAPTER SEVEN

FAIRCHILD

EARLY MORNING. Mid-southern latitudes.

Dani opened her eyes, squinted at the brightness that had crept over the far, eastern horizon, and groaned loudly to herself.

"Pain is an indication that you aren't dead, dear," Eleanor sang out with that extra-bright and positively happy voice she usually reserved for especially-bad-hangover mornings. "Time to rise and shine and take on all that a strange, alien world has to offer, Ms. Crusoe. Or should that be Madame Dantes?"

Dani refused to be drawn into whatever game Eleanor was playing this morning. She presumed the names were literary references of some sort. Eleanor was very much a reader of old books.

The thought of spending hours with her nose tucked into a book filled Dani with an existential dread so great she decided to immediately add another tattoo to the collection of icons and sayings liberally distributed under her flight suit, just as soon as she got back to civilization and could find a passable dive with a needle artist.

However, instead of grumbling, or going back to sleep, Dani sat up and popped her back and neck. The ground was hard and uncomfortable, but at least she was dry and warm.

"You sound like my mother," Dani grumbled, mostly to herself.

"That might explain why you never listen to me," Eleanor retorted. "Perhaps I should have your father reprogram me to look like one of your sim stars when we return to Panamuer Nuevo? Some beefcake stud with long, flowing hair and a six pack. You might pay attention when he tells you that you are about to do something stupid."

Dani picked up the Aide box from where Eleanor had been sitting on a handy outcropping of stone, just so she could stare into the woman's eyes.

"Do you really think that would help?" she asked acidly.

"After this many years with you?" Eleanor smiled back, just as tartly. "No. Not really."

"Good," Dani smiled and tucked Eleanor into her pocket as she stood up and stretched to loosen everything. The sky was amazingly bright this morning. "What's first?"

"You need energy and water, dear."

Eleanor even sounded like a Governess this morning.

Having a rambunctious eight-year-old charge in a thirty-one-year-old body probably contributed.

Dani sighed. Qunsahr Industries Emergency Pack, it was.

She always tried to pretend that the emergency survival pack she wore on her back didn't exist. Today, reality refused to comply. She reached back and unsnapped the fabric pouch from her kidneys and pulled it around front where she could see inside.

One quick zip to open it and she nearly dumped the entire contents on the side of the mountain, so Dani crossed her legs and dropped in place, holding the little, ballistic nylon purse in her lap so she could root around inside.

There. Ugly square lumps, hooked together, small enough to fit in her palm and about half as thick as a deck of cards. Three of them. Blueberry Scone, Strawberry Shortcake, Oatmeal Raisin. Compact energy bars made by the lowest bidder and routinely thrown out uneaten and replaced at the end of a twenty-five-year shelf-life.

This set still had eight to go.

Yummy.

Dani pulled the Blueberry Scone loose and noisily tore its wrapper free from the other two. She said a small, personal prayer to whatever gods of birds and sailors might save her from having to try one of the other two tomorrow. She might consider human sacrifice to avoid eating them.

She popped up her face plate and took a bite. The smells of this planet were odd, and hard to identify, but the bar overrode everything with a taste like wet cement.

Industrial, flour-based cardboard populated by the occasional colored nugget of chewy, manufactured as cheaply as possible in response to regulations. At least it wasn't completely desiccated. Dani chewed like her mother, her flesh mother, was watching a recalcitrant five-year-old at the dinner table with Brussels Sprouts.

The first bite was unmitigated hell. The second was chewing nettles and barbed wire.

Somewhere around the third bite, her taste buds apparently decided to commit mass hari-kari. She stopped tasting anything and only registered the texture, and was able to chew through the bite and swallow past a barely-resisting throat.

Dani heaved a heavy, put-upon sigh.

"At least you have the ability to experience true sensory input, dear," Eleanor observed tartly.

That brought Dani back to herself. The AI did have a point.

Water next. Her suit had about two liters of fresh water in pouches along her ribs, below her breasts, and would slowly process sweat and urine and everything else into more, given time, but she would need to add to the equation, especially if she had jarred her helmet enough to kill the radio. There might be a slow leak up there bleeding moisture.

The gadget in her hand looked like a gray hat, rolled into a tube, with the word *Water* written on the outside in fourteen different languages. Dani unrolled it flat down her thigh and located the friendly 'Pull here' tab located near the suddenly-exposed nipple. It came free and revealed a nifty, little ideogrammic explanation.

Pulling the strip exposed a battery lead to complete a circuit inside. Over the next twelve hours, a small osmotic generator thingee would pull water vapor out of the air and force it through some filters and into the canteen, like the belly of the small, brown narwhal, if you looked at the nipple like a horn.

Once live, it would continue to automatically refill the pouch until the battery drained, somewhere in a month or two, depending on use.

It wouldn't be enough to sustain her in a climate like this for all that long, but her life-support system would keep moisture in just as well as air, so she wouldn't dry out nearly as fast, and her helmet had the right plug interface to use the narwhal's horn, if she turned her head just right.

Good enough for the rule of threes. You could go three minutes without air in space, but she was on a habitable planet. Three hours without heat, but this was a warm planet, even at night. Three days without water, but she should be good for months at this point. And three weeks without food. Dani was tempted to try, given how nasty the protein bars tasted.

What else?

Some purification tablets she could drop into uncertain water, if she ever found any, and some energy drink mix she could add to the canteen for flavor.

Another small, vacuum-sealed pouch had survival clothing: floppy hat, blanket, spare socks, leggings, shirt, and rain poncho. Opening the air seal would cause them all to undergo some strange, chemical expansion that made them stop being doll clothes and fit her, but she wasn't in a hurry.

The small medkit got her attention, but she didn't crack it open yet. It would just be the usual stuff: disinfectant, bandages, staple gun, and sanitary wipes.

Next to that was the tiny, green bag she was dreading the most. Maybe even more than eating another energy bar. It had her name printed on the side in big, pink letters and a date when she had last stocked it.

Dani was one of the three percent of women allergic to the drug Velomear and all of its close copies. Every single one of them. Almost every other woman she knew got a shot once a year that completely suppressed her menstrual cycle so they didn't have to go through it until they were ready for children.

For Dani, every month felt like a return to barbarism.

There would be the drop in neuro-chemistry as her body prepared to host an egg. Then the day that the egg passed. Two days later, the craziness of the pre-menstrual cycle, only tempered by the joys of modern medicine, but still causing her to drop into a soft case of OCD behavior for a day or so. And then several days of leaking blood.

In Dani's case, the custom free-glider suit had been specifically designed and built by two women in the University of Palomar's bio-engineering department. It could handle all the excess drainage, with a modification to the normal pee cup to handle fluid overload.

The suit also had a device in the crotch that she thought

of as a harpoon gun, specifically built in so she could deploy an absorbent cotton tampon without getting naked first, and then later retrieve it, even in the vacuum of space.

Her egg had passed yesterday. The clock had started.

If she wasn't back to civilization in four days, Dani would probably have to break open that bag and enjoy all the dread pleasures of hunting the great, red whale.

She needed to find something to take her mind off the messy, bodily activities coming up.

Ah, there you are.

Down at the bottom of the little satchel were the two things she really wanted to play with. One was a survival knife with a hollow handle filled with all sorts of neat things, but she would never get them packed again if she unscrewed the pommel with the compass and dumped it all out right now.

We'll just leave well enough alone, thank you.

The other one was more fun, anyway.

The Tomya Manufacturing, Ltd. Survival Tool looked like a nifty, slate-gray, beam pistol because it was easier to hold and point that way. Inside the body were four micro-flares. The grip held enough fire extinguisher for about ten seconds. There was a can opener and a bottle opener on opposite sides of the barrel.

But the best part was the signal laser.

You could twist a nob and set it to a super-powerful flashlight, or a short-range cutting beam, or a medium-distance fire-starting laser. Not that she had any wood, but pyromaniacal tendencies wormed their way deep into your soul and never really get exorcised, no matter what lies you told your shrink.

Dani pulled the Survival gun out, pointed it at some rocks, and made sure she could set things on fire if she needed.

Or if *ennui* set in.

The holster had a tape backing, so she peeled it and stuck it to her thigh where it would be out of the way but still accessible. The survival knife scabbard went on the other leg.

She would look kinda silly, if she had to fly, and it would mess up her aeronautics a little, but nothing would come loose and she could adjust.

And it made her feel like an action hero from a vid-sim, all set to take on space pirates or something.

Dani pulled out the last item at the bottom of the pouch with a tablespoon of dread. She had been putting this part off, mostly unconsciously, hoping that the world would get magically better before she got to this point. But it had not.

One small box, about the size and weight of a deck of playing cards, themselves a unit of measure older than space flight.

Qunsahr Industries Emergency Radio.

Ultra-high tech, bleeding-edge sophisticated, radio-satellite pocket comm. Rugged and water-proof. Reliable, dependable, reassuring. Supposedly indestructible.

Whoever had originally designed it had not taken into account Escudra VI. Or, at least, this part.

She didn't even bother trying to turn it on once she pulled it out. The smell had already given things away. Her radio reeked of smoke and strange, organic chemicals.

Dani guessed, from what little engineering know-how she had picked up, that the storm had caused the device to ground internally and overcharge the battery. That had been the sweet, sickly smell she had picked up when she first opened the emergency bag. Some kind of battery acid leaking.

The side of the radio was already discolored and bulging slightly. Dani didn't think that was even possible until now.

She sat the little device down on the same rock that

Eleanor had kept watch from all night and stepped back, just in case the damned thing exploded in the next few seconds.

"Oh, dear," Eleanor observed. "The radio would appear to be somewhat less than operational, wouldn't it?"

Dani did a double-take and looked down down at where Eleanor could peek out from the pocket. She could never tell when the Aide was being serious or extra sarcastic, even after all this time.

Dani settled for a noncommittal grunt.

Morning. Halfway down a mountain.

Dani knew where east was.

She had been north of Beta when all hell broke loose, although there was no chance she could manage to walk there from here, even if she knew where there was. It was probably at least one hundred kilometers from here, and she had no idea where it was without all her electronics.

Good enough.

Dani picked out a spot to her south and memorized the landscape around it, so she could zero down on that as she walked. It was green, a bit. Not much, but better than the various hues of rock and gravel and mountain available at this elevation. Maybe fifteen kilometers over, and several hundred meters down, once you accounted for all the wrinkles and bubbles between here and there.

On a regular planet, downslope would be where you found water, and plant life, and civilized people. Hopefully, Escudra VI would be no exception.

Dani could not, for the life of her, remember anything about the briefings on local fauna or flora. Probably doodling at the time.

That meant that none of it was that dangerous, right?

Whatever. She had the survival gun set to fire-starting mode. That would do in a pinch.

Dani took her first step when Eleanor spoke.

"Dear?"

That was it. Nothing else. Not much more was needed. They knew each other too well.

"Downhill. South. Hopefully home," Dani replied.

"I see."

Eleanor was usually not one for such pithy brevity. But Dani agreed.

Not much to say at this point.

"Might I suggest an arrow in the dirt?" Eleanor said.

"A what?"

"Scuff your feet in the dirt to effect a discoloration," Eleanor explained. "Shape it like an arrow, pointing in the direction of travel, large enough to be seen from an overflight."

Right. Survival school 101.

Dani could tell she was rattled that she needed to be reminded of things that should have been automatic.

But then, she had never been shot down over enemy territory before, either.

Dani eyed the ground and began to shuffle.

She really needed to pull herself together.

CHAPTER EIGHT

CHIKE

HE WOULDN'T HAVE BELIEVED it, not without incontrovertible proof.

Chike continued to walk around what had been a clean camp three hours ago. Now it looked like the morning after a frat party that had been busted by the cops at the wrong moment. And he had been at a few of those.

The tents had all held their structure, in spite of the electrical surge that had overloaded equipment, but the Convention Center had a nearly meter-tall drift of sand piled against the windward side, like the aftermath of a blizzard. All the other tents were in various states of disarray as well.

Three of the personal tents had collapsed, but otherwise held, so he was dealing with panic and shock rather than burns and broken bones.

At least the rest of everything was relatively clean. The winds had scoured every loose piece of paper and biodegradable food wrapper and carried them away, never to be seen again. Archaeology for future generations to uncover.

Everyone was outside, picking up overturned tripods and righting communication and sensor masts.

Hadley had claimed a portable picnic table and sat with a handful of undergrads around her, heads together with a lot of gesturing and pointing at slabs.

Ann-Marta approached now with a look of rueful disbelief on her normally-composed face. Only the twinkle in her warm, brown eyes gave it away.

"There will need to be new procedures implemented, tomorrow," she commanded in a low voice as she walked close and turned to face downwind with him.

"Oh?" Chike inquired carefully.

Serious Ann-Marta was dangerous Ann-Marta. Dragon Ann-Marta.

"Somewhere between one-sixth and one-quarter of all the electronic gear we had set out beforehand is gone."

"Gone?" Chike asked, aghast.

"Gone," she repeated, gesturing at the long meadow that lead down from this plateau. "Picked up by the genie and carried away. I presume we'll find most of it out there over the next few days. Lord only knows how much has survived."

"Wow." Chike let that sum it all up. Even the storm on Riggel III hadn't done nearly that much damage.

Stakes would be set deeper tomorrow.

Ann-Marta was a stickler for those sorts of details. If her strict Camp setup procedures had failed, he could only imagine what the normal scientific camp would have looked like right now. Nobody else he had ever worked with was this careful.

Probably anywhere else would be a warzone.

"Mostly, deeper mast-poles and secondary cable-loops," she continued. "I'll chalk some of it up to haste in pulling everything out so you folks could go mass-science mode on the fly. But still."

Chike let the silence hang for a moment as he considered the probable debris field.

As a xeno-geologist, there was nothing for him to do as part of the overall cleanup. He was really just in charge right now, at least as much as Ann-Marta would let him be. There were other experts, like Hadley, who would dig into the operational details and equipment logs for answers. His job was to provide direction, guidance, and arbitration.

"Search and Rescue time?" he asked finally.

"Yes," Ann-Marta agreed. "But first, we need to thoroughly check out the wingsuits to make sure they have not suffered any malfunctions or degradations from the storm. I'm not about to send Fahmida or Juan-Marco out there and then need to turn around and rescue them as well. Plus, the sun will set in another ninety minutes. I'll send them up at first light."

"No signal from Fairchild?"

Chike felt the first pangs of nervousness. He liked the crazy pilot. It was unimaginable that the odds had finally caught up with her.

Chike had a hard time thinking of any other person he had ever met who was more alive.

"Calypso has an emergency beacon triangulated," Ann-Marta said quietly. "Roughly one hundred kilometers north-northwest of here. Says that the shuttle craft hit hard."

"Hard?" Chike probed.

"Straight-down, angled slightly backwards for the wind. Free fall," Ann-Marta continued. "I'm working on the presumption that Fairchild lost all power up there and bailed out. She would have."

"So we just need to backtrack from the wreckage?" Chike felt the first glitter of hope.

Jumping from the shuttle into that storm would have been insane.

Right up Fairchild's alley.

Hell, she might turn it into a sport on this planet, if left to her own devices.

If she had survived it.

Stop thinking like that. She made it out fine. You'll find her soon.

You did not send her to her death.

"Something like that," Ann-Marta agreed with a growl. She was in full-on Viking bad-ass mode now. Going to jump in her longboat and go loot Ireland, or something.

"And it will probably take Giles six to ten hours to get the backup shuttle ready to fly?" Chike guessed.

"Call it a whole day before they can land here," Ann-Marta growled. "Longer if we have them do any sort of search pattern before they come for my people."

Her opinion of the operations staff on Calypso was much lower than his. But then, she tended to run an entire crew of long-serving, planet-side experts on missions like this, rather than relying on undergrads looking for experience, credits, or a good time, like the academic side of the Expedition did.

She rounded on him suddenly, that Viking glare taking over her whole face, her whole body.

"What's the weather forecast look like?" she said.

"Hmm?"

Chike was a little lost.

"That storm was not on the briefing materials," she continued. "I would have planned better. What are the chances it happens again in short order?"

Good question. Frightfully, bloody good question.

Rather than speak, Chike strode forward suddenly. He had the correct expert sitting thirty meters away, probably discussing that very topic, if he knew her.

Hadley was facing towards him as he approached, one silent eyebrow up. The rest of the small group fell silent as

Chike's shadow fell across them, the chocolate Viking a stride back and to one side, like a dragon on his wing.

Chike suppressed a grin at the image.

Serious business. Or something to that effect.

"Ann-Marta had an interesting question," he announced. "How soon until we see another one of those storms?"

Hadley smiled like she had just won a bet with the students around her. Knowing that woman, she probably had.

"Scientific Wild-Ass Guess time, Dr. Odille?" she smiled up at him.

He nodded. Her SWAG was still going to be better than anyone else's. Probably by orders of magnitude.

"This terrain favors the formation of big storms," she said. "Warm, moist air gets funneled in from the west by a slowly converging pair of low mountain ranges. When it hits the bottom of the bottle, there is nowhere to go but up, causing the storm to form and drop whatever rain it had. At the same time, winds from both northeast and southeast swirl in on this side of the ridgeline, adding to the instability and drying out the remaining air. Throw in the right temperature differentials, and odds are you get a big storm fairly often. What I don't know is the surface geology over there. What causes the electromagnetic surge?"

Yes, what would?

All dust storms created a static charge. It was in their nature. This one had gone off the charts, suggesting something magnetic in the dust itself. Chike slid onto one end of the bench, sat down, and leaned forward to think, elbows on the tabletop and chin on fists.

They had only barely begun to scratch the surface of Escudra VI, as it were. It was an Earth-like world with a water cycle, a plant/oxygen cycle, and killer-awesome lightning storms.

The dust under his elbows got his attention.

Chike blinked in surprise.

He had been thinking in terms of iron, such as made up the core of the planet. The gold-pink hue of the dust piled everywhere suggested something more interesting.

Chike reached back and cursed under his breath that he had left his portable laser spectrometer back in his tent instead of in a back pocket, where it normally lived.

When in doubt, fall back on the ancient methods, as his first professor of field surveys had always said.

Chike grinned at the weathermen around him and licked the end of his right index finger. He ran it across the dirty, scarred picnic table top in front of him, picking up a thin film of that pinkish, goldish dust. He stuck his finger in his mouth and tasted the sand, treating it like a good wine.

Everybody else blanched in shock.

Nobody ever said geologists were sane people.

"I'm guessing you have an oxide of copper in here, bonded with something else that makes it a little less stable and a little more conductive, as well as change the color from the deep red it would be, were it pure," Chike replied to the shocked student with a smile. "I'll run it through some tests this evening, but let's assume that any storm in the vicinity will conduct a static charge at higher than Earth rates, as a starting hypothesis."

He rose and nodded, his face threatening to break into a massive grin at the open mouths and wide eyes around him. Only Ann-Marta was cool, but she'd seen him pull stunts like this on unsuspecting undergrads before.

"I'll get someone to run it all through a mass spectrometer tonight and have you a breakdown in a few hours."

Or he might do it himself. Hadley Swain wasn't the only

person who might end up writing award-winning papers from this planet.

Chike winked at Ann-Marta as he turned. She had the decency to not roll her eyes as she turned to follow him away from the sudden gabble that had broken out at the table behind him.

"So now what?" he asked, after the two of them had moved off a bit. In places, it was like walking on a beach now, with soft, gritty sand blown everywhere over what had been reasonably-packed soil yesterday.

"Food for my crews first," Ann-Marta countered. "They'll be up early getting everything organized and setting out to look for Fairchild. Your kids will be up all night going through logs and samples, so they can be fed later and won't want an early breakfast. You?"

Chike nodded. She had done this before. And she was still in charge, until they rescued Fairchild, or at least located her.

"Off to brief Giles, and maybe snag some coffee," he said. "And then I owe Hadley a readout so she can plan for the next storm better. You suppose we should move the camp farther out?"

"No," Ann-Marta said decisively. "If Fairchild comes this way, she needs to be able to find us. We weathered the last storm just fine. By end of day tomorrow, we'll come through an even bigger one like that without any trouble, now that I know what to expect."

Chike shuddered at the thought of another one like that. While the mass spectrometer was running, he planned to see if the automated survey stations had picked up anything like this over the last few years.

Escudra VI had always promised to be interesting, especially in the quest to find artifacts or concrete evidence of the Elder Race. He wondered how such a race would have responded, but nobody had ever been able to even prove they existed, except as a result of all the terraformed, inhabitable, and empty planets humans had found to their liking in this corner of the galaxy.

At least Fairchild wouldn't have to worry about little, green men.

He hoped.

CHAPTER NINE

FAIRCHILD

WALKING DOWNHILL WAS a lot harder than it looked. Or maybe, Dani hadn't walked a significant distance by herself in a long time.

You could always take a taxi to the club, or catch a ride with a friend. Something.

This putting one foot in front of the other for hours was a total bummer. Absolutely useless, because there wasn't even a nice drop-off she could use as a ramp to throw herself into the sky and catch some thermals or something so she could glide there.

No, just this stupid mountain.

God, her feet hurt. And her calves. And her thighs. And everything else.

But that spot way over there wasn't going to magically fly over and meet her.

Dani knew she was lazy, but damned if she wasn't more stubborn.

"So," Dani said aloud, hoping for something useful in the way of conversation.

Even getting lectured by Eleanor was preferable to the silence in her own head.

"Are there any alien remains on this rock?" Dani continued.

Eleanor grunted in response. After this long, that was a placeholder while the AI Governess tried to decide if Dani was serious, or just grumbling, and how much of an answer to provide.

"No," Eleanor finally granted. "All evidence suggests that Escudra VI will be as empty and bereft of signs of intelligent, star-faring aliens, as every other planet human have yet explored."

Really? None?

"Why not?" Dani asked after a bit. The joy of a conversation with an AI was that long gaps could pass without words. Eleanor might grow bored, but she was already thinking at several times Dani's speed, so she might not even notice.

"Do you remember The Fermi Paradox from school, dear?" Eleanor asked in a nice voice.

So, not a lecture. Or, at least, not a hectoring one.

Anything to break up the monotony of walking down a soft slope towards a bunch of rocks that didn't seem to be getting any closer.

"Let's assume I slept through that lecture," Dani said.

It was a safe enough assumption. She had always been able to study the night before a final for a couple of hours, maybe skim through a textbook or two, and ace the test. Not that she retained any of it for more than week afterwards.

But that wasn't her problem.

"So in the Twentieth Century, a scientist named Enrico Fermi famously asked the question *Where is everyone?* at the point where astronomers could scan the heavens with advanced, technological systems, looking for signs of intelligent life."

"They weren't there," Dani replied. Everyone knew that.

"Correct," Eleanor agreed readily, settling her tone into schoolmarm mode. "Since humanity has begun to explore the nearby galaxy, there have been no intelligent life forms located. But there are a large number of worlds that humans could inhabit with only minimal adaptations."

"Not seeing it, yet," Dani grunted, concentrating on not flipping ass over teakettle over a large rock outcropping as she walked. Her legs were killing her, but she was *really* tired of this mountain and wanted off.

"So all theories suggest that there should be intelligent life out there, dear," Eleanor continued. "Somewhere. And many of these worlds bear evidence of terra-forming, that is, being artificially altered to make them habitable, mostly by introducing simple, DNA-like life forms that would establish the carbon, nitrogen, and water cycles necessary to sustain biospheres."

"How long would that take?" Dani mused aloud, forgetting that she had an audience. Or a witness, depending on how you wanted to interpret it.

"The current estimates range from ten thousand to over one hundred thousand years, dear, depending on the level of technology evinced by these theoretical beings commonly referred to simply as *The Elder Race*," Eleanor answered. "For scale, that is from before iron became a human tool, back to almost as long as we have existed as a species."

"Wow," Dani said. She had to stop as a rogue thought threatened to make her brain explode. "So where are they?"

Again, the pause. Probably rendering it down into simple soundbites. Eleanor certainly knew her charge.

"There are three theories. Would you like to hear them?"

Is that better than hours of silence, broken only by the crunch of gravel? Are you stupid?

"Yes, please," Dani said finally, politely even.

Not really, but seriously, better than being alone in her own head.

"First, they might have retreated from the galaxy, possibly to a homeworld somewhere, and continue to live quietly," Eleanor continued, her tone floating back and forth enough to actually keep Dani enthralled, something few professors had ever managed for long.

"Second, they died out, either of old age or internal warfare. This theory has less proponents, because there would be an expectation of ruins, none of which have ever been reliably identified as old enough and the product of intelligent life."

Huh. Yeah, imagine finding my room a thousand years from now, with empty and decayed food wrappers, half-full bottles of whiskey, and dirty clothes. Proof of intelligent life? Something, anyway.

"Lastly, they simply evolved beyond a merely material form and decided to clean up after themselves before they left, like good galactic stewards."

"What?" Dani blinked hard. "Like gods or something?"

"Who knows, dear?" Eleanor responded.

"Wow," Dani repeated. "So what makes this dry, desolate rock so interesting?"

Again the pause.

"Just tell me, Eleanor," Dani snapped at her. "I'm smart enough to understand. Most of the time I'm just too damned lazy to care. But right now, I'm stuck out here with nobody to talk to but you, so I need some damned thing to keep me stimulated."

"Well," Eleanor replied, a shade frostily. "Since you asked so nicely: the terraforming on Escudra VI seems to be failing.

If Dr. Jones-Parker and Dr. Odille and their teams can understand the rate and possible acceleration of that failure pattern, they believe that humans can use that as a reliable timetable to estimate when the Elder Race left."

"Shit, really?" Dani was aghast. This was real science, not just tinkering around with wells and excavations. Big stuff. Important things.

Way more interesting than just flying a shuttle into storms and orbital insertions for money. Maybe she should have paid a little better attention to the briefings.

Or something.

"Have they found anything?" Dani finally asked, aware that Eleanor was ignoring her random outbursts. Did AIs get bored? Miffed?

Eleanor had certainly been programmed to imitate stubborn, but how much of that was real? How much of her Governess was just an incredibly sophisticated computer program, reacting to external stimulus within known response patterns?

But then again, how much was Dani?

It is better to remain silent and be thought a fool...

She bit her tongue before speaking out loud and damning herself for all eternity. Eleanor was probably a better human, a better person, than one Danielle Cooper. Certainly to speak from experience.

And she was trapped in the middle of an alien planet right now and couldn't go get drunk to wash away the memory of self-realization.

This sucked.

One foot in front of the other. One boot forward, then the next.

Keep the eyes down and then up and then down. Scan the horizon, scan the path. Look for rescuers, try not to faceplant on stone.

"At present, they have not," Eleanor said out of the blue.

"Not what?"

Dani was lost, then realized that Eleanor had answered Dani's question, albeit after a gap of thirty seconds.

"Not found any aliens, artifacts, or signals indicating such aliens existed in a recent timeframe," Eleanor said.

"Define recent," Dani stated, aware that she sounded like a barracks lawyer looking for an out, something, distraction before she wandered down into her head and got trapped.

"The last major Ice Age ended on Earth approximately twelve to thirteen thousand years ago, and lasted for well over one hundred thousand years before that," the Governess responded smugly, obviously waiting for that question.

Dani was beginning to think she was getting predictable. Never a good sign.

"And how long have we been around?" Dani hesitated, afraid she might learn something today. Also, probably never a good sign. Pretty soon, she'd be using her brains to solve problems instead of her cute butt.

"Anatomically modern humans date back approximately two hundred thousand years, dear," Eleanor said. "Theories of the Elder Race posit that they left the galactic scene around one hundred thousand years ago, plus or minus fifty thousand."

"And the farthest edge of the galaxy from here is only seventy-five or eighty thousand light years from here," Dani observed. She did pay attention to the finer details of astrogation. Anything dealing with space. "So any signals they may have sent have probably long since passed us by and evaporated into deep space."

Dani hadn't realized that an AI Governess could gasp in shock until she heard the sound emerge from the pocket on her chest.

"I'm not stupid, Eleanor," Dani growled, hurt and little defensive. "Lazy, but not stupid."

"No one ever called you stupid, dear," the Governess replied. "Your father doesn't count because he was angry at you and said many things he really didn't mean."

No, he probably did mean them, knowing Alphonse Cooper. Dani couldn't say.

She had been in deep space for as much as she could of the last four years, except for occasional forays home to visit her siblings and spoil her nieces and nephews. That way, visits didn't involve her going to the family estate and getting into any more screaming matches about bad choices and embarrassing the family.

For a moment, Dani wondered if she was better off never returning to Panamuer Nuevo. She could make a really good living as a test shuttle pilot on these expeditions. Had, for several years. Had flown through some crazy shit and done some amazingly stupid things. Seen far more of the galaxy up close and personal than she ever had on tours and going all walkabout with a credit card.

As long as she didn't have to actually grow up. Never going to happen.

"Dani?" Eleanor asked carefully.

"I'm fine," Dani said, suppressing tears of frustration as well as tears of rage.

"I can tell that from your voice," her oldest friend in the universe said sarcastically. "Look at me."

Dani took a deep breath and pulled Eleanor from her pocket, bringing the woman up so they were face to face for the first time in several hours. It was usually better to just pretend to be on the comm with her, than to have this woman watching her face.

It was hard to hide secrets from Eleanor.

"I'm sorry, Dani," Eleanor whispered. "I really am. I wish there was something I could do to make it all better."

Dani shrugged. She had grown used to being shallow and a little vapid.

It made the world hurt less. Most of the time.

Dani shrugged again. She didn't trust her mouth not to betray her at this moment.

There were a lot of angry words bottled up. Had been for a long time. Usually hidden beneath alcohol and bad behavior.

Irresponsibility.

Except when she was sitting in the cockpit of a flying machine, making it dance. Maybe that was the way forward? Pretend to be flying more often, and approach the rest of life like that?

Of course, that required far more sobriety than had been her acquaintance for many, many years. She'd probably go into withdrawal if she went dry.

Still, maybe it would be worth it.

Stupid had gotten her here in the first place, after all.

"I'll be fine," Dani announced to the world. And to Eleanor. And herself.

She found her jaw hurting and realized how hard she had been grinding her teeth for the last five minutes, or hours.

"Are you sure?" Eleanor ventured.

Dani tilted her head up and stopped walking. She took a deep, angry breath and let go of it. Of the angry, of the resentment.

Nobody was responsible for her being here. Nobody but herself.

"Yeah," Dani said quietly. "Yeah, I think I am."

She looked around, turning to trace her track backwards up the slope and then down to that spot where she hoped to camp tonight.

"How are we doing?" she continued.

"Another two hours should see us to a better spot," Eleanor replied. "Perhaps close enough. Your eyes are better than mine."

"What do the records say about life forms on this world?" Dani asked.

"Why?" Eleanor teased. "Tired of the energy bars already?"

"Nope," Dani replied. "Don't want to be eaten by dragons or bears or anything."

"Your guess is as good as mine, dear," Eleanor snarked. "We should cut another arrow, so the search parties can find us."

Yes. Good idea.

Assume success. Plan for victory.

Stop and shuffle an arrow in the semi-loose rock and soil, ten meters on the long axis and hopefully obvious enough for whoever ended up flying the backup shuttle down to rescue her.

Maybe it would be Rain. She could use a friendly face right now, and he might be willing to give her a roll in the hay.

That felt like a really good way to affirm being alive.

Dani wasn't sure she ever had wanted so hard to be alive.

CHAPTER TEN

CHIKE

MORNING.

Chike had managed to sleep. Some. Enough. Probably.

The laser spectrometer runs had thrown up as many questions as they had answered. And promised at least two really good articles in prominent, ancient, Earth-based, scientific journals. Probably at least one more geology-meteorology-centric survey Expedition to Escudra VI, if he wanted to lead one. Or come along with Hadley when she completed her doctorate and came back.

He looked at the readouts again and whistled to himself in the privacy of his tent.

A variety of oxides of copper, with some iron, some aluminum, various arsenides, some more exotic metals, and a bunch of other things generated by some noisy, recent supernovae in the vicinity, baked in the core for a few epochs and then tossed skyward by drift and tectonic pressures.

Not quite a room-temperature super-conductor, in their raw forms, but certainly a live, copper wire, lying on the desert floor, just waiting for a good storm to come along and toss it into the air with a little lightning.

Interestingly, had the initial storm been smaller, the damage to the camp would have probably been far, far worse. As it was, the winds had blasted through everything too quickly to cause all the buildings to revert to transport mode. Add a few grounding cables in the right places, and some better insulation on others, and most of the gear would not have overloaded and reset.

Chike could just imagine the smile on Ann-Marta's face as he gave her the equations. Her people would tear into the bar stock and carbon rods with a vengeance, fashioning new toys. He wondered if she would trademark everything and turn around and start selling improved gear to other survey teams.

Maybe Escudra VI was going to make all of their careers.

Now, they just had to bring Fairchild home so they could complete the fairy tale.

Chike transmitted a quick summary report to Ann-Marta's inbox, slipped the laser spectrometer into his back pocket, where it had worn a faded pattern into the fabric, and folded up his slab. The weather promised to be warm, bordering on rudely-hot in a few hours, so he had worn a thin, gray jersey pullover with a kangaroo pouch in the front for his slab, right below the Michigan State logo and the Spartan helmet on his chest that matched the tattoo on his bicep.

Giles had done his undergrad work at Ohio State.

The Convention Center was a throbbing mess of people coming and going, even worse than the showers. There were far more academics than he was expecting, since the sun had barely been above the horizon for an hour at this point. He wondered how many had simply been up all night and were grabbing breakfast before sleep.

Chike filled his Spartans mug with coffee and located Ann-Marta, seated in a corner with a couple of people that looked like ex-Special Operations types: hard, rugged, tough, dangerous. The two guys were almost as tough looking as Ann-Marta and the other woman.

Chike slid onto the end of the bench next to a man who had at least an entire head of height on him and twenty kilos of mass, all of it muscle. Always useful to have folks like that around.

"Dr. Odille," the man nodded with purpose and a serious smile belying the flattop and close-cropped blond hair that screamed ex-military.

"Morning, y'all," he replied.

Ann-Marta already had her nose buried in her slab, reading. She looked up with a fierce grin on her face, like she was about to sack some unsuspecting fishing village just appearing from out of the morning fog.

The woman could be really, really intimidating when she got locked in on something. It was a good thing she was such a pleasant bridge partner.

"Thank you," she said to Chike with a happy smile, almost a purr of excitement.

He watched her transmit the file on and turn to the woman across from her, on the other side of the guy next to Chike.

"I'm sending you Dr. Odille's preliminary findings," Ann-Marta said. "Round up the machine shop folks and get them in motion as soon as you can."

"On it," the woman rose in one smooth motion, unruffled cup of coffee in one hand and disappeared at a fast walk.

And just like that. It was kind of unfair, considering the number of meetings and approvals he would have had to undertake to accomplish big things, and nothing would have happened in a hurry. Here, aim the Ground Services folks at a problem and get the hell out of their way.

Which is why he always hired Ann-Marta or one of her friends for the job. Better to have reliable professionals.

"So what's the news?" Chike asked, sipping a mouthful of hot, bitter coffee to try and cut through the gunk that seemed to be coating his brain this morning.

"We expect the second Shuttle groundside in three hours," Ann-Marta replied. She gestured at the men remaining at the table. "Gavin and Lacumaces will head out with it at that time and coordinate the search. Fahmida and Juan-Marco were on site at first light and have been flying search patterns, but the radio interference in the area has been almost thick enough to cut with a knife."

"Back to primitive methods?" Chike asked.

He wondered how long he would have been able to survive a hostile planet alone. Everyone else at the table probably would have gone months, or maybe years.

He gave himself days.

"Maybe," Ann-Marta replied, glancing at the two. "You two should go get packed."

Both men nodded, excused themselves, and vanished in short order.

She stopped and studied his face closely.

"I've got good people, Chike," she continued. "We'll find her. I'm more worried about storms."

"I thought you would be able to harden the camp to survive them," Chike said, maybe a little put out.

He had stayed up way past his normal bedtime tracking down all the science so she could fix everything. A little credit would be nice.

"And we will by mid-day," she replied. "The problem is that another storm might come up in the same place, and we would have to either retrieve all the S&R teams on short notice, or send them up to Calypso to ride it out. I will not have people on their own out there in something like that."

"Can we put a search base somewhere closer?" he asked.

"I thought about that, Chike," she mused. "The problem is that they would have to be a goodly distance removed from the epicenter, so we don't really gain anything, and end up with more places that need to be secured and protected."

"So what can we do?" Chike heard his voice starting to take on a childish whine, but he couldn't help himself. He was supposed to be in charge of the Expedition while it was on the ground.

Being powerless was frustrating, even with Ann-Marta to take the sting out of it. Where had all this guilt and defensiveness come from?

"If she's not dead, and not hurt, it's just a matter of finding her," Ann-Marta reassured him. "Needle in a haystack, but we have our ways."

Chike felt at least a little relieved.

Hopefully, Fairchild was sitting on a rock somewhere waiting.

Knowing the pilot, probably sunbathing nude on a north-facing rock slab and complaining about how long it was taking for them to get there.

CHAPTER ELEVEN

FAIRCHILD

"I THOUGHT you said there were no aliens," Dani whispered harshly as she scampered for cover into a little draw that looked like a dry creek bed. They were still above what she would have called a treeline, so there was little cover except for strange looking cactus kinds of plants, all spiky and green and round.

"What I said, dear, was that humanity has encountered no intelligent, star-faring aliens in our explorations." Dani could tell that Eleanor was a bit put out, just from the tone of exasperation pervading her voice. "I did not say there were no lifeforms on this planet."

"So what the hell is that?" Dani kept her voice quiet, but couldn't keep the adrenaline out of it.

"If you would lean back, or take me out of this pocket, I might be able to answer you better," Eleanor retorted tartly.

That would involve taking her hand off the fire-staring laser in its holster, or climbing up on her knees so she wasn't bracing her weight on her left hand. But it was probably a smarter move, considering who the expert on native fauna probably was on this team.

Dani settled for rolling onto her left hip, elbow down, so she could kind of pull the Aide out and rest her, face up, on the rock ledge, pushing with one, long finger to get her Aide's balance far enough out that she didn't slip back. The right hand was all set to draw and fire if that thing got any closer.

"That appears to be a very large raptor, dear," Eleanor said after a bit. "Not one that I can find in my data files. Perhaps you will have the opportunity to name it when we get home."

"Name it?" Dani blinked and looked down at Eleanor's face for a moment, before she turned her eyes skyward again.

That thing had to be big, to be seen from that far off.

How big?

"It is customary to have the person who discovers a new species provide the common name and the taxonomic classification, once it is determined to be a previously-undocumented species," Eleanor said smugly. "Fairchild's Golden Eagle, perhaps?"

Fairchild's Golden Eagle? That actually sounded kinda cool. She might have to paint that on the side of her next Survey Shuttle, just to show off. Every ship needed a name.

Right now, however, she was more worried about the possibility of being eaten. That thing looked like it had a four or five meter wingspan. Creature that large could probably take down bighorn sheep, maybe just lift them into the air so it could drop them and make them dead, like birds back home did with oysters.

Dani pulled out the Tomya Survival Tool and checked the beam setting. Sure enough, set feathers to flaming at close range, assuming the damned thing came down to take a swipe at her. She wasn't taking any chances.

The bird had circled once in the sky, a single, majestic orbit, and now seemed headed off on a tangent, but Dani wasn't fooled. She had played enough war games on flight simulator computers certifying and retraining for shuttles. Circle around and come up on them like a ninja from out of the sun.

If a golden eagle like that was really that big, she would be able to give Dani grief if she wanted.

Plus, what did a bird that big eat? What size of ground creatures was she likely to find this high up in the mountains that might feed a bird like that?

Dani stirred herself, realizing that Eleanor was awaiting some sort of answer.

"Yeah, maybe," Dani finally agreed. Fairchild's Golden Eagle sounded good, at least for now. "I wish I had a pocket on my back where you could ride and keep an eye on it. I would feel better if we were below the tree line, but we're in a desert and there are no trees. Not even big cactuses."

"Cacti, dear," Eleanor corrected. She did that. "If you turn me around and hold me down at your side when you walk, I should be able to watch the skies behind you."

Not optimal, but better than nothing. Dani waited until the giant bird had truly disappeared before she moved again, like a rabbit frozen by the owl's call and hiding in the brush until it was safe.

Not a pleasant feeling.

Dani wondered how the bird would react to her flying around with it.

She shrugged and turned completely in place once to make sure where she was.

Somewhere above her, the spot where she had woken up. Somewhere above that, the rock that bore an imprint of her helmet. Below and ahead of her, a valley was starting to open up. At least, a notch in the mountains around her, so hopefully a place where a river existed, even a creek, and she could hang out.

Eleanor had dutifully reported that Escudra VI had things close enough to trees to count. Dani could maybe rummage up some downed trees and build a little shelter. Start a fire to keep the night terrors at bay. Maybe even spend some time outside her suit and do a little maintenance on it so it didn't get all funky and stuff.

And a nice fire would generate a column of smoke that ought to bring folks running.

Anything to keep from having to eat another protein bar.

When she got back to civilization, she was absolutely throwing out most of the emergency pack she had and rebuilding it with some expert assistance. Starting with palatable food.

"What does this rock have for lifeforms?" Dani asked in a truly querulous voice.

Before, she had been talking to talk, lest the silence sneak up on her and drive her into her dark places. One of the downsides to having a regular, monthly cycle was that day when she could easily fall into OCD. Dark, angry places where she might be trapped for a day or more, unable to overcome her own brain's neurochemical squishiness, looping endlessly on some trivial thing and unable to think happy thoughts.

Just leaking blood was a godsend compared to that, since she could think objectively again by that stage.

Now, Dani found herself confronted by the possibility that critters down here might be big enough, hungry enough, to chase after her, even if she had almost no smell because of her life support systems.

Secretly, Dani wondered how many had missed her last night while she was unconscious, unable to smell her. Certainly, the shark in her dreams had swum by instead of biting her.

"According to the logs, not much is known," Eleanor

responded after a few moments. "Most of the surveys had been done at much lower elevations and closer to the equator. Ground Station Beta was chosen as a survey site on the general assumption that there were very few lifeforms in the area, and thus the crew would have more security. Plus Dr. Odille is a xeno-Geologist and Volcanologist, so he was planning to emplace a number of big, sciency-type instruments to measure the mountains themselves, rather than the fauna that might walk atop them."

Silly boffins. Always focused monomaniacally on the task at hand without any thought to what else the world might offer. Sounded like someone else Dani knew, but she was unwilling to speak aloud.

"So, Fairchild's Golden Eagle," Dani hazarded. "What would an eagle that size eat?"

"I've been giving that some thought," Eleanor replied in a subdued tone. "If we scale up from similar raptors on Earth, I would guess very large lizards or small ungulates. Or the planetary equivalent thereof."

"Define small," Dani said in a small voice. She had a pretty good guess at the answer, but wanted someone else to say it first.

Eleanor was silent for too long.

"Probably ranging from forty to seventy-five kilos, depending," Eleanor finally said. "I'm sorry."

At fifty-two kilos, most days, Dani was, too. Then she reset the Tomya to use the short-range cutting setting.

If that bitch grabbed Dani from behind and swept her into the sky, there would be two surprises.

One, Dani would cut her heart out with the laser first. Two, Dani would circle her falling corpse as it hit the ground. Laughing, and probably using the other setting on the Tomya to set her feathers on fire as they went.

CHAPTER TWELVE

CHIKE

IT WAS ANN-MARTA'S SHOW. Chike was just along for the ride at this point.

Everyone else had been chased out of this part of the Convention Center, the primary conference room, except him and Ann-Marta. Only Hadley and her team of undergrads were even still in the building at this point.

The big screen on the short, gray wall had been split into four views to project the maximum amount of information. Top left was a view from Fahmida's helmet camera. Top right was the same thing from Juan-Marco. Bottom left was a zoomable satellite map with topographical overlay being updated in almost real time by the smart systems in the radio hut. Bottom right was a real-time view from orbit after Calypso had deployed a stationary weather satellite and zeroed it in on the area, so they could track for more storms, smoke, or dust, before something snuck up on them.

They had nothing.

Well, absolutely stupid amounts of useful data about weather conditions transmitted from the two wingsuits, as well as much finer detail than had previously been available on the terrain and topography.

But no Fairchild.

You did not kill her. You just haven't found her yet.

The Survey Shuttle seemed to have landed more like a leaf than an arrow, possibly buoyed by its lifting surfaces, even without power. Fahmida had even landed briefly and climbed into the wreckage first thing this morning. All she had found was some kind of bright blue fluid, hydraulic or insulating, leaking into the landscape, and a hole in the upper deck, right where the ejection seat would blow Fairchild clear of the dead craft to the safety of an electromagnetic dust storm.

Looking at the wreckage from up close cameras, Chike had been amazed that the hull was still largely intact. He had assumed that a shuttle falling out of the sky without power would have been crushed like a beer can being driven over by a tractor trailer. This one even looked salvageable, one of these days, if they could fly a dry-dock lifter out there to pick it up.

Or maybe hire in some rednecks from one of the crazier towns back home to come in and fix enough systems that the thing could manage orbit on its own, where it could be flown to a repair yard.

"So now what?" Chike asked quietly.

Ann-Marta had been hunched over a standing microphone, speaking quietly to both wingsuit pilots, who appear to be enjoying themselves soaring over the desert and mountains.

"Now? Patience," she replied with a tight smile. "Small needle. Big haystack. We know roughly where she bailed out, but a free-glider can go a long ways in the right wind. Lord only knows where she might have ended up. I'm guessing we'll need to fly a search pattern about sixty kilometers across, elliptical on account of the winds, and then track down everything that looks interesting. It would have been nice to fly some unmanned craft, but there is already such a tremendous amount of static charge in the atmosphere from the storm. I'm not sure any of them would make it home."

"Is there anything I can do?" he asked in frustration, staring down into his empty coffee mug, as if the grounds would tell the future.

Ann-Marta smiled serenely at him.

"Organize the undergrads to clean everything up?" she offered with a sly smile. "Help cook lunch? Go commit science so this planet doesn't sneak up on us again? This is just going to take time. You'll know five seconds after we find something. I promise."

Chike rose from the bench with a grumble under his breath and headed towards the front door. Waiting was driving him to distraction, but he couldn't help himself.

Planetologists didn't do emergencies, or fast. Even earthquakes and volcanoes gave warning, if you were listening.

"Dr. Odille," someone yelled from outside as he emerged into late morning sunlight. "Shuttle coming in."

Okay, that he could help with.

Chike pulled out the comm from his other back pocket and listened as the incoming pilot talked to someone on Ann-Marta's Ground Services team, plotting wind, elevation, etc. All the mundane things that got a big, burly Survey Shuttle from orbit to ground without damaging anything.

Three minutes later, the ungainly bird was settled on a pad well away from camp.

Chike found himself vibrating with nervous energy that had no useful outlet.

Rather than wait, he hitched a ride out with members of Ann-Marta's team to service and inspect the gray bird before themselves joining in the survey. Those folks rode everywhere in the camp in a little open-framed, four-seat, four wheeled jitney with a pickup bed on the back.

Right now, he was in the front seat, with the two men from this morning's breakfast, Gavin and Lacumaces, sitting behind him, with their own oversized backpacks tied down in the bed.

The driver was a tiny woman who drove the little cart like a pack of hungry wolves was chasing her across the desert. Chike hadn't gotten her name, but he was very glad he had listened to her quiet advice to strap himself in before she powered it up.

She might have stopped to pick him up if one of those lurching bumps had tossed him out the doorway and onto the side of the road. Or she might not have and then come back for him when she was done.

He wasn't willing to put odds out and test theories. There were limits to his scientific bent.

Calypso's secondary, backup Survey Shuttle was still going to be warm to the touch, but not hot enough to burn, as long as you were smart enough not to lean against one of the leading edges that tended to get red hot during reentry.

The craft itself looked like a very-stubby leaf spear with a main deck that had loading ramps at both front and back, nestled between the two mammoth engines that rested atop a big delta wing that sloped down ever so slightly while it was at rest. The pilot sat in a small, glass-sided chamber at the front of the Shuttle, up a level from the cargo deck, like an old-school aerial fighter craft from an earlier century, where she could see all the way around herself while flying.

Rain was flying today. He didn't rotate evenly with Fairchild, taking perhaps one flight to the ground to every three or four of hers, mostly because the pay was the same and Fairchild wanted the stick time more than he did.

Rain was a seriously laid-back dude from the eternally gorgeous paradise of eastern Australia, somewhere close to Sydney, originally. Laconic probably would require too much effort from the man.

Rain walked down the rear ramp and sauntered in Chike's direction, dressed in comfy shorts, a Hawaiian shirt, and combat boots. He had long brown hair, rather like a rock star than a hot-shot pilot, and stood maybe a quarter head taller than Chike, so maybe a meter-eighty-five or a meter-nine.

"Did an overflight on my way in, Dr. Odille," Rain announced as he got close. "Just in case. Didn't pick up any radio signal, but I was barely able to find the landing beacon here until I was almost on top of it."

"Thank you," Chike responded. "So what's the next step?"

"Have you ever done one of these before?" Rain asked.

"No," Chike left it at that. He had never lost a pilot before, or any other staff member that had gotten farther away than the radio contact necessary to guide a team in and the embarrassment on pulling them out.

"So there are two flyers out there now," Rain said. "Chances are, they won't see anything. But they're not supposed to. Somebody reviewing their footage here, or one of the smart systems, might see something. We might as well, since I can hover on thrusters way better than a wingsuit can roll tight orbits around a spot on the ground. Either way, we get close. Either I land, or drop a jumper out the back ramp who can soft drop and identify whatever it was we saw."

"So you have done this before?" Chike asked. That actually relieved him, that he might be theonly virgin around here when it came to this kind of operation. Not that he was interested in becoming an expert.

"Usually civilians back home," Rain smiled. "I'm also

rated on all helicopters and most fixed-wing aircraft up to four engines, so I occasionally fly Search and Rescue missions for the local constabulary, wherever I'm at on Earth. I prefer to fly Survey Shuttles because the pay is so much better. Flying anything else is expensive. Gotta pay for my hobbies somehow, you know?"

Chike smiled up at the man. That would explain Fairchild. She lived to fly into space and back, far more than aircraft, preferring to let someone like Rain taxi her up to altitude in her free time, so she could jump out and free-glide in. He wondered if that made them a better team. Certainly, he had never even heard rumors of Fairchild being involved with anybody on either crew: Calypso or Expedition.

"I understand, Rain," Chike said. "How long until you head back out?"

"Oh, five minutes," the tall man replied. "Mostly, just letting them get organized and packed away, so nothing flies out at low altitude when we're overhead. You going to fly with us?"

Chike was torn. He was supposed to be in charge of Ground Station Beta, but Ann-Marta exercised Executive Authority until the emergency was over. The grad students were organizing the undergrads. Ground Services was organizing everything else. He was way too frazzled to handle the delicate task of setting seismographs for a baseline.

And he couldn't cook.

Would anybody really miss him?

You know what? There was a time to stop being the stuffy academic and let his old, juvenile delinquent tendencies come to the fore. Again.

"I hadn't planned to, Rain," Chike decided. "But I think I will. Not going to jump out, but I can at least ride shotgun with you and monitor the sensors. If anybody needs me, they can call on the radio anyway."

"Sounds good, Dr. O," Rain held out a hand that Chike shook. "Welcome aboard."

Chike found himself trailing the big, rock star pilot up the rear ramp and into the shuttle's cavernous hold. Fairchild's craft had seemed so much smaller when it was packed with forty-odd people and all their gear. On this trip, the inside of a shuttle was almost a cathedral.

Chike followed Rain up a small side staircase to the flight deck and watched the man strap himself into the big chair in the middle of the room. Chike grabbed one of two matching support consoles, in this case, the one on the right, closest to the stairway.

Space was at a premium up here, even as big as the shuttle was, so he had to kind of shuffle along, but he was able to slide his station's chair out on rails, fold himself into the seat, attach every strap, and then rail himself forward.

Fairchild had taught him, early on, to hook every strap and keep it tight, and to keep coffee in a bulb with the top closed. That she had done it the hard way just made it a lesson he was never, ever likely to forget. Kind of like the woman who had driven him out here ten minutes ago.

While the pilot faced forward from a small dais, the other two stations were down, below the level of the windshields, and tucked into the corners of the otherwise oval-shaped control room. On a clock, Rain would face twelve, while Chike was at four.

He powered up the station and logged himself in with the override code that let him do pretty much everything except fly. The autopilot on a bad day was still light years better than he was, but very few people knew their way around a database or firmware bios system better than he did. While Rain went through his pre-flight checklist, Chike established a set of search parameters that took into account a person as alive and crazy as Fairchild, and set it to poking through all the imagery from everyone looking.

Ann-Marta might have thought she was conservative in setting Fairchild's possible flight distance within a sixty kilometer ellipse. Chike knew the woman better than that. He had the system start at the outer edges of Ann-Marta's search grid and go out another forty kilometers, and then run a secondary sub-routine to stay very close to the exact center of the storm itself.

Not where the shuttle had crashed, but where the sky had fallen in.

Fairchild was a bird. Chike needed to think like one. Either she had ridden the wavefront until it died down, or, more likely, she had set her teeth into the wind and free-glided all that mad energy in not-much-more than her naked skin.

Seriously, once Fairchild figured out how to do it, Chike fully expected to see her free-glide in nothing more than her squirrel wings, and maybe, just maybe, enough of a bikini that none of the sensitive bits got wind-burned. She would want to feel the wind on her skin.

"Ground Station Beta, this is Calypso-2, cleared for takeoff," Rain's voice intruded. "Flying three."

"Who's your third, Calypso-2?" Ann-Marta's voice came back instantly.

Chike heard the man laugh.

"Dr. O, you want to answer or should I?" the pilot called across the meter or so of space, rather than using the internal comm.

Around them, the shuttle rumbled at an ever louder rate as Rain put power to the thrusters and got air beneath them.

At least Rain wasn't going to make him get off. The least Chike could do was handle one grumpy Ground Services Coordinator.

"Beta, this is Chike Odille," he said solemnly into the radio. "I'm the extra passenger on Calypso-2."

There was a pause, probably filled with a string of very colorful profanities at the other end of the radio.

"You couldn't resist, could you?" Ann-Marta finally said. Her tone might not be enough to polish granite, certainly it could knap flints.

"Sorry, Beta," Chike said with a rueful smile. "I can't cook."

That got a laugh.

"Fine," Ann-Marta replied in a voice wavering between angry and teasing. "But keep your radio open, in case someone needs to find you. Otherwise, I'll have to bring you up on insubordination charges."

Which, in Ann-Marta's case, would be two or three weeks of kitchen duty, cleaning pots and helping the actual cooks get their jobs done. Something to be avoided, since the cooks would all be in on the game with her.

"Acknowledged, Ann-Marta," Chike said over the roar of the engines.

At least out there, maybe he could make a difference.

CHAPTER THIRTEEN

FAIRCHILD

OKAY, so maybe she would call it a tree. They looked kinda, sorta alike, anyway.

Maybe kissing cousins.

Dani didn't do botany.

The tree thing was three times taller than she was, and kinda woody. Maybe tree-ish. There was a definite trunk that emerged from the ground and branched out into secondary and tertiary pieces as it got a meter or so off the ground. The skin looked like her Aunt Trudy, who was really, really old and wrinkled. Plus the woman had strange, brown spots that none of the other women in the family had. Trudy, not the tree. Well, the tree, too.

Dani had similar spots on the backs of her hands, so she suspected that Aunt Trudy just happened to be the only honest one in the family about what she really looked like.

Aunt Trudy truly didn't give a shit what her brother thought, or any of the rest of them.

Some of that might have rubbed off on Dani.

Just saying.

Trudywood? That might make a nice name for strange,

alien trees. The weird little branches, like Trudy's hair, poking out everywhere with ten centimeter thorns just heightened the similarity with Aunt Trudy.

Dani could also see little burrows or something, inside the ring of thorned fingers that came down to the ground, pointed outwards, so she assumed critters about the size of small rabbits lived there. She had paid enough attention in her biology classes to know that the tree wouldn't put up with that unless there was some sort of symbiosis thing going on.

Probably rabbit turds as fertilizer, or something. They go out at night and eat things. Bring the nutrients back and poop them everywhere for the tree to absorb.

Crap, at this rate, I'm going to turn into a scientist. Can't have that.

I'll blame everything on Eleanor. After all, they'll be her pictures, right? I'm just the pilot transporting the soon-to-be-galaxy-famous Governess/Scientist around while she conducts her fascinating explorations.

Yeah, nobody's going to buy it. I'll have to sweet-talk one of the boffins into coming up here and taking all the credit.

Hmmm? Which ones were cute enough to sleep with, to convince them to fall on their swords and write up these findings for her and take all the credit?

Dani giggled madly to herself before she could control it.

"Yes?" Eleanor asked drolly.

Dani lived in perpetual fear that her Governess could actually read Dani's mind. Then they'd both end up in the looney bin. Or jail.

Take your pick.

"As long as you promise not to tell," Dani replied slyly.

"Need I remind you, again, dear?" Eleanor seemed to be on the verge of rolling her eyes so hard she might pull something. So, business as usual. "I am generally legally prohibited from disclosing personal information about you, much like the traditional attorney/client privilege. I have to know of an actual crime before I can even offer data, and even then it must be done under a valid court order."

"Yeah, I know," Dani retorted. "There are reasons I occasionally stuff you in a pocket backwards, or leave you on a bathroom counter, you know."

"Just so we're clear," Eleanor stated unequivocally. "And why are we giggling today?"

Dani lifted Eleanor up so she could see the thorn bush clearly.

"I have no interest in conducting the sorts of rigorous, scientific field studies of the native fauna that might burrow inside and flourish under such a flora," Dani said. "Let alone positing and testing theories of symbiotic relationships between the disparate life forms, to say nothing of writing up academic articles for journals back home."

"I see," Eleanor replied carefully. "And what made you giggle?"

"Trying to figure out which one of the biologists I would have to seduce to get to come down here and do it for me."

"Oh, honey," Eleanor's voice suddenly got all sultry and stuff. "All you have to do with a xeno-biologist is whisper the words *new animal species* in their ear and then make sure they don't run you over in their mad rush to get there first. Any seductions at that point are merely a cover on your part, as we already knew."

Dani raised a finger and started to argue the point, and realized that Eleanor was right. She almost shifted fingers.

Boffins just weren't like her other friends: the pilots, the daredevils, or the trust-fund-dilettantes. The kind who were beginning to get a little stale and possibly predictable, now that she thought about it.

Probably just too *White Picket Fence* as they got older.

Not that academics were exciting, but they were certainly excitable. Inspired. Mad for the possible discoveries and wholly concentrated on it. Perchance infectious in their enthusiasm to learn new things and truly understand how the world worked.

As opposed to people from her other life, where lately it had been one round of rather dreary dissipations and parties after another. Profound disappointment, as the body slowly burned out the right receptors and the old standbys just weren't enough anymore. Then it became necessary to up the voltage, running harder just to stay in place.

Dreary. Tedious.

Mundane.

Crap, I'm growing up. And nobody stopped me, you bastards.

"However," Eleanor continued. "Perhaps Milo would be a good candidate. He's a smart one, and rather nice. And he has a nice butt."

"Rawr," Dani agreed. It was a very cute butt, attached to a lanky, ex-basketball player from someplace boring in Europe. Switzerland, maybe? Sweden? S-word of some sort, she was sure.

And it would probably take a lot of effort to convince him. Dani was looking forward to all the time and attention it would require, climbing him like a squirrel with a particularly-tasty tree, just to bring him around to her way of thinking.

After all, what good was science without a really good romp along the way? And he would owe her, big time, for such an opportunity.

Dani grinned and licked her lips.

She turned slowly in place, memorizing the landmarks she could see from here so she could guide her intrepid, and hopefully appreciative, boffin back here later.

And to make sure that damned Golden Eagle hadn't snuck up on her.

Nothing. Good.

Dani decided that this was as good a spot as any to take a break. It was almost local noon, from the elevation of Escudra VI's sun, although the definition of an hour was different here.

This planet rotated slightly slower than Earth, but everyone had long-ago agreed to maintain a standard, twenty-four hour clock, based on sixty minute hours and sixty second minutes. And then slicing the planet into roughly-equal time zones so people could localize.

You ended up adjusting the definition of a local second up or down to match the reality of local noon and local midnight, with *Zulu*, your Prime Meridian, generally being derived from the point of First Landing.

Since Ground Station Alpha was a quarter of a planet away, everything was calculated from there.

And without electronics in her Heads-Up-Display, Dani could only guess at the actual time, but she was within thirty minutes of noon, one way or the other, which was close enough. She really needed to add some old-school non-electronics to her kit bag when she got home. Maybe a mechanical wristwatch like however many-times-great-grandmothers might have worn.

Her brother Rudy, with his fascination for antiques, would be the perfect person to ask when she got back.

The water bottle had been slowly inflating all morning. Dani decided to pop her face-plate up, at least long enough to smell the area, and so she could take water straight from the nipple, instead of having to kind of turn her head sideways in her helmet and stretch her lips out to dock.

Escudra VI was fully habitable. She could have probably stripped down to her flight boots, and the emergency pants and shirt from her pack, maybe chopping those pants into capris or shorts. But then she would have had to carry the suit with her everywhere. Awkward, if not all that heavy.

Better to find a spot near a lake or river or something, and then strip naked and let the sun worship her. Like all men should.

Escudra VI had a dry smell. Dusty and rich, almost like freshly-baked cinnamon bread mixed with a tangy something that reminded her of the time she had stuck her tongue to a battery to test the charge.

Almost citrusy, for lack of a better term, at the back of her tongue.

Happily, she hadn't crash-landed in a swamp. Not that she was aware of any within a thousand kilometers of here, but those places stunk, no question about it.

No, she could handle this. If it hadn't been so dry, she would leave her face-plate up all the time, but she needed to retain as much moisture as she could for now, and breath and sweat were fantastically bad ways to dehydrate yourself in a hurry.

Nope, clamshelled up for now. I smell pretty good, all by myself, at least for now. Probably get funky in about five more days, so we need to get rescued before then.

And preferably before the harpoon gun became necessary in another seventy-two to ninety-six hours.

Ugh.

Dani had been still and quiet for so long that a furry, little head popped out of a burrow and looked around. Short fur, somewhere between salmon pink and burnished gold. Two enormous eyes. Cute, pointy, bunny ears up and ratcheting around like radar dishes.

It dropped from sight as soon as she moved.

Dani circled the Aunt Trudy tree carefully and found a dead version of the tree a few decameters beyond it where the main trunk had fallen over and provided a something like a bench, upon which she could plant her butt for a little while and let her feet rest.

The local equivalent of ants had something like ten legs, instead of six, and moved slower, at least right now. Dani pulled out the Tomya and dialed it to fire-starter mode, just in case any of them decided to get frisky. They might not smell her, but many creatures reacted to vibration instead. And they might bite.

Dani stayed at her end of the dead trunk and put Eleanor between her and bug-land like a chaperone at a teenage party.

Four hours of walking so far, mostly downhill or flat, across rough terrain that frequently alternated between giant slabs of exposed stone and puddles of gravel. But she was starting to get to places with soil.

Everything around here reminded her of the northern Sahel, on Earth, arid plains slowly giving way to grass and shrubs.

At least everything growing was some variant of green and brown. Dani decided she probably couldn't have handled anything verging over into the cotton candy, kids' cartoon worlds, or some of the better places she had experienced on man-made pharmaceuticals.

This was just Utah. She could do Utah. Hell, millions of people did every year.

Piece of cake.

Dani let Eleanor watch the bugs while she examined the slope above her.

She figured she had covered around six kilometers by now, possibly eight, since she hadn't been pushing herself to get anywhere except to a lower elevation. She was pretty sure that her starting point this morning had vanished from sight, up over a ridgeline somewhere.

It hadn't been obvious from above, but she could see ripples in the rock now where she had come down, like waves on a beach. Probably, she had dropped at least three hundred meters in elevation as she had walked, as well.

Need to cut another direction arrow.

In a few minutes. Resting, thank you. Feet hurt.

Patches of greenish grass blades were starting to emerge as the ground got softer, competing with nasty, littler versions of the Trudywood trees.

Yup. Sahel. Right at that point where the Sahara starts to fade into the savannahs of Central Africa, but hasn't made up its mind yet.

Suck down some more water. Contemplate really, freaking big raptors and little bunny rabbits.

Dani wondered if the rabbits here could be eaten. Not that she was desperate enough to find out, yet, but she was in the middle of nowhere, had no radio, and could only guess when, or even if the boffins back home would find her.

Plus, emergency food bars.

Escudra VI was a really, freaking big planet, to go with really, freaking big Golden Eagles.

Dani muttered a prayer to the patron saint of shuttle pilots, liberally mixed with profanities derived from six languages, and threw herself to her feet. For the briefest moment, she considered setting fire to some of the trees around her as a way of signaling the rescue teams where she was, but managed to contain her inner pyromaniac.

Trees might burn. Hopefully, the forests around here contained enough lignin and other nifty things that she could burn them. However, she had no idea how hot and fast they might burn.

That sandstorm had been amazingly normal, right up until the moment when Escudra VI decided to get weird and toss a forcefield-grade electromagnetic pulse thingee at her.

Perhaps it would be better to gather up some smaller bits of wood and make sure they didn't explode when exposed to heat?

Crap, now I really am starting to sound like an adult.

Dani nearly lit the whole damned forest on fire in frustration.

She could see the fire in her mind. Smell it. Taste it.

Her heart ached for it in ways that would make the White Picket Fence boffins back at camp probably faint. Her jaw ached from the way her teeth were suddenly grinding.

She raised the Tomya and aimed it, fingers slowly squeezing enough pressure into the trigger button to make it all go away.

"Fairchild, dear," Eleanor's voice intruded. "Is that wise?"

Something broke inside Dani. Ruptured, like a spent water balloon.

She sagged and nearly fell over as her muscles unlocked.

Dani sucked a hard breath in, feeling the lock of sudden tension across her neck and shoulders, like an army of angry pixies stabbing her with those cute, little cocktail swords that bartenders stuck through fruit when you ordered something floofy.

Wise? No.

Necessary? Possibly.

No, that was the chemical imbalance in your brain speaking. That dark bitch in your soul snuck up on you early this month. Thought you wouldn't notice her coming in through the bathroom window and taking over the joint.

Thought she could make you really crazy this time, instead of just a little nuts.

Thought she could finally own you.

Dani slid the Tomya back into the holster on her right thigh with hands that refused to stop shaking. She clenched them into fists and turned back to face Eleanor, unsure what to say in response.

"It's bad," Dani finally blurted out.

"I know, Dani," Eleanor replied warmly. "I could tell. Let's cut another arrow and then walk some. Exercise usually helps you focus."

Dani strode over on wobbly legs and scooped Eleanor up, carefully reversing the woman in her grip to watch backwards before holding on for dear life, her one, true friend in the cosmos being a computer program who was programmed to keep the *tendencies* at bay, under control.

Safe.

Dani found a spot with a nice amount of clearing and set to work shuffling her feet through the dust and growing layers of dirt. This one would be extra-large, compared to the rest.

Dani had nothing to hide behind. No booze. No drugs. No mindless, casual flings with strangers to protect her from that dark patch that lived at the bottom of her soul.

She would be alone out here, but for Eleanor to keep her sane. At least until the rescuers showed up.

They had better hurry.

CHAPTER FOURTEEN

CHIKE

"SO WHAT DO YOU THINK, Dr. O?" Rain called above the soft roar of the engines as the Calypso-2 Survey Shuttle orbited the wreckage site slowly in a clockwise pattern.

What did he think? Why the hell was he up here, instead of back at camp being in charge?

Because he wasn't in charge. He was just getting in Ann-Marta's way and probably annoying the hell out of her and her people with his pestering questions.

At least she was used to it, hopefully, by now.

It was the scientist in him, forever asking *Why?* to the world around him. Geologists were supposed to be patient creatures. He got that. He didn't get patience when there were things to do. Dragons to slay.

Princesses to rescue.

Not that Fairchild qualified as a princess. Well, maybe a little, considering who her father was, but he wasn't supposed to know that. Nobody was. She was *Fairchild*, not Lady Danielle Cooper of Panamuer Nuevo.

If she wanted to make her way in the galaxy and hide the

fact that her father probably could have bought Calypso outright from spare change, who was he to gainsay her?

She was also a damned fine pilot.

Chike just wasn't used to yelling above engine noise while flying. Fairchild would have used the internal comm. But then, she would have been wearing that blue bodysuit that looked skintight, stretched over a frame that was all muscles instead of curves, with a helmet that had all the electronics built in.

Rain took an entirely different approach to flying. Chike could see him buzzing sea lions for fun, just to see if their eyes really had whites.

"I think that I needed this trip," Chike finally ventured, daring to speak the words out loud, where Ann-Marta wouldn't hear and razz him mercilessly for months.

He glanced over a shoulder to see Rain smiling down at him from the pilot's seat, like a deity offering a blessing.

Chike's shoulders had come down. He couldn't think of another way to describe it. The tension had bled out of his neck and back as he headed into the sky. Not that he expected to be able to do anything, but just being out here was enough.

Helping.

The mountains kept drawing his eyes, but that was the geologist in him. He could read the history of the world in the bones he could see, upthrust and breaking through the skin of Escudra VI.

She was an old world. They knew that. Drier than Earth, too, but there was evidence else that she had been cooler and wetter in her youth. Or perhaps, middle age.

Habitable was not her natural state.

Earth had long-ago evolved creatures who respired oxygen into the early planetary atmosphere, setting the stage for larger and more advanced life-forms to appear and eventually dominate over the course of the last half billion years.

Escudra VI had been a rock with a dead, rather boring atmosphere, for much of her life. Not as thin and empty as Mars. Not as exciting as Venus. But not a place where life had evolved that would look up at the stars in wonder.

Something had happened. Or rather, someone had happened.

Humans had found any number of rocky worlds in the giant sphere they had explored slowly outward from Earth. Many of them were habitable by humans. Pleasant even. The right gravity, within a few percentage points. The right atmospheric balance of oxygen, nitrogen, and trace gases. All the little lifeforms that sustained the carbon lifecycle. Some of them were even edible, which said something, given the wide availability of amino acids upon which life itself could be based.

But here, on Escudra VI, all of that was a frosting added to the world at a later date. Almost yesterday, geologically, compared to the stack of bones in front of him.

To everyone with half a brain, that argued for someone, the cake-makers who had originally made the world habitable. Yet they had left behind no evidence of having been here, except for these worlds.

To the more religiously minded, that reminded people of the old biblical line about having many rooms in his Father's house, and the exploration age had created a renewed interest in religion, driven by a warm, charismatic Patriarch who preached a message of divine forgiveness and the importance of second chances, after all the damage humans had done to Earth along the way.

Some called them Archangels, showing the path.

Scientists had generally agreed to the term Elder Race, working on the presumption that they had existed once, but had disappeared. Truly, it was a mystery, to find worlds with evidence of terraforming, but no terraformers.

No monuments in orbit, all carefully placed where only space-traveling wanders would find them. No Sentinels on the Moon watching.

Nothing at all out of the ordinary.

Except Escudra VI, where the terraforming appeared to be failing. Where the Elders might not have been omnipotent, after all. Where maybe, just maybe, they hadn't quite cleaned up after themselves.

Who knew?

Maybe they had been in a hurry to leave. Maybe something had happened.

Chike didn't know, but was intent on finding out.

What would it be like to finally find someone else out there? To know we weren't alone? To touch the face of God, as it were?

The alternative was an even worse thought.

To have missed them, by however little, and be left to face the darkness alone.

Geologically, Escudra VI was an old world. But that layer of frosting over the top was only perhaps a million years old, at most. A soft, candy coating. The thin flesh of a plum over a very large, very hard stone.

Had the Elders left so recently? Had they predicted humanity? Could they have? Or were there other children yet to be found, still lost in the darkness, awaiting their turn?

"You're quiet, Dr. O. Find anything?"

The sudden interruption scattered Chike's mind like a wind into fog.

Rain. Flying. Rescue mission.

Fairchild.

Chike brought his concentration back from the wool-gathering places where he had wandered off to.

"No, Rain," he yelled. "Just thinking far-too-serious thoughts down here."

"Understand, Dr. O," the pilot called back. "Gavin wants us to land so he can start a mechanical inspection on the other shuttle. Wanna walk around and stretch your legs?"

"That would be marvelous, Rain," Chike decided.

He was not an adventurer, but here he was, having an adventure. Geologists set up their gear with precision and then went back and watched the readings from a safe place. Or rather, they sent grad students off to supervise undergrads, into the cold, wet, and miserable, and let them do the work while the professors, like Chike, got most of the credit.

It wasn't fair, but that was the way of things.

If something bad happened, it tended to happen to other people.

Chike knew part of the reason he was here was a layer of smothering guilt over what had happened to Fairchild. Flying the storm had been his call, a chance for some really solid science right at the beginning of the ground mission.

Nobody could have predicted that outcome. But he should have known.

Chike was going to have another hard night sleeping, unless they managed to find her today.

Or recover her body.

Chike didn't want to think about that.

He had already freaked out a little when Fahmida had first reported liquid seeping from the downed shuttle this morning. Being bright blue had only partially restarted his heart from that place where he had been expecting to have to take charge of transporting a body home.

That would have been another first, and one he would be happy never having to deal with.

Ever.

The engines changed camber around him, vibrating at a higher pitch as the shuttle slowed and began to hover downward on thrusters. The landing gear deploying sounded like a bank robber trying to pry open a safe with the world's biggest crowbar. Touching down was like being in a car having to stop suddenly, as Chike was thrown against the seatbelts holding him in place.

He truly appreciated how easy Fairchild made it look, when he had to fly with other pilots who lacked her deft touch.

At least the engines were powering down. They were on solid ground.

He could go look inside the place he had been originally thinking of as Fairchild's tomb.

He could do this.

Outside, the sun was getting hot. Or he had spent too much time in air conditioned huts and ships, and not enough in the open air.

One of the perks of being in charge was sending other people out in the nasty stuff to do things. That brought a smile to his face.

The mid-day sun was bright in an empty sky. The grit was dry and itchy.

Calypso-1 was not scattered all over the landscape as his mind kept expecting. It was, in fact, still in one piece, even. Broken and dented and absolutely not flying again, any time soon, but intact.

Part of that was the soil around here. Instead of striking a solid rock surface, the shuttle had fallen into a large notch, almost a little valley, which appeared to be filled with sand and a soft layer of goldish soil.

A number of plants had been crushed underneath the weight of the craft, sticking out in all directions or broken off and scattered. But still, that had provided something of a mattress to jump on.

Chike followed Gavin across the open space, leaving Lacumaces and Rain to rest in the shade of one wing and drink some soda pop from aluminum cans.

Calypso-1 wouldn't hold air, getting into orbit. That much was obvious from the way the back ramp was ajar in its cradle. While the flight deck could be sealed off, Chike doubted that any pilot would trust that, relying on a flight suit. He wouldn't have.

The sand and dirt here was almost white in places, fading to only barely golden-brown at the darkest. Except where a thick drip of bright blue sludge was slowly oozing its way down from the shuttle and puddling in a low spot.

He would have worried, but Ann-Marta had explained to him this morning that the hydraulic fluid was derived largely from a gelatinized ethyl alcohol that was only slightly more intoxicating than water, and which would bio-degrade with barely any trace if left exposed to the elements for a month. So he wasn't going to poison the soil around here, and probably not the local animals either.

Getting gophers drunk didn't count.

Chike followed Gavin in through a side hatch and onto the cargo bed floor. Other than being slightly torqued out of shape, the door had even opened under power with a little prying from a bar Gavin had brought along. Upstairs, the now-open skylight let in dust and grit, with the pilot's station empty and both side chairs still in place.

So, she had ejected. Hopefully safely. And was out there somewhere, needing the rest of them to come to the rescue.

It was one thing to hear those words. It was something

else to actually stand here and understand what they meant. To touch this place with his own hands.

Chike had needed to see this, to know this.

He could do this.

Downstairs, he found Gavin waist-deep in a side panel, presumably inspecting the engines. Or maybe the hydraulics system, since that had appeared to have been the original failure.

"Gavin?" he called, waiting for the man to pop a head out of the panel and turn to face him. "You'll be safe here alone?"

"I'll be fine, Dr. Odille," the man replied. "You won't be more than ten minutes away if I need something."

"Okay," Chike didn't know what to say.

He wouldn't find it that easy to just rough camp somewhere at the drop of a hat, but that was part of what made Ann-Marta's team so good. And why he hired them for his Expeditions.

Chike wandered outside and looked around. Once Gavin completed his inspection, it might be worth moving a small portion of Beta's crew and staff up here, if Calypso-1 could be made to fly again.

Then he remembered where he was, and why the shuttle had crashed in the first place. There was no way in hell he would put any more of his people at risk than he absolutely had to.

Chike stomped back over to the other two men, more angry at himself for even thinking it.

Those men were relaxed and smiling as he approached, but sobered quickly under the withering snarl he felt pasted to his face, even as he tried to calm himself down. All the mistakes to this point were his fault, not theirs.

"Anything the matter, Dr. O?" Rain asked carefully.

"No, Rain," Chike replied. "Mad at myself. Let's go find Fairchild."

He went past the men and up the ramp of the other shuttle craft.

Calypso-2.

Into the belly of the beast.

CHAPTER FIFTEEN

FAIRCHILD

"HOW ARE YOU DOING, DEAR?" Eleanor asked her in a simple voice.

Dani stopped, looked around, and took a deep breath before she answered.

The walking had helped. It let her grind the repetitive tendencies in her mind out into something useful.

At the same time, the enforced silence had set her to circling the outer edges of her mind, like her shuttle falling into a nice equatorial orbit while she chased down her mothership. Except that the mothership was always staying a step ahead of her, no matter how hard she ran after it.

It was worse than the teenage dream of walking through your school naked as a jaybird for all the world to see. Nudity had never bothered her. Physical nudity.

Emotional nudity, psychological nudity; that was something else.

Dani didn't do quiet. Not without starting to climb the walls.

It didn't matter that the only walls around were in her head.

"Holding it together, for the most part," Dani replied finally.

It was an honest answer.

"I've been walking backwards for an hour," Eleanor said. "Where are we?"

Dani turned Eleanor around and panned the area in front of them.

The terrain Dani had been following had narrowed down considerably here as it wound around the mountain. Peaks on three sides of her established a bowl with a big notch chopped out of the north side. Not the direction she wanted to go, eventually, but she was getting to a lower elevation, so on balance, it was good.

On any other planet, this would be a river bed. She could still see the remains of something that running water had cut, once upon a very long time ago, over the course of several centuries, to measure the layers of ground excavated from the sides of the slopes next to her.

The pathway, what might be equitably called a valley on another planet, had narrowed as well, until it was maybe only one hundred meters across the flat spot, at the widest, sloping away backwards. Not quite a defile, but not the open areas of the morning. It was still Utah out here, with clumps of Trudywood trees growing a little bigger now, and a lot more frequent, mixed in with things that looked more like a cactus was supposed to.

Birds were getting to be a little more common as she got lower, but these were smaller ones. Honest-to-God hawks with a wingspan no wider than her own. Hunters that might bother her rabbits, but would leave her alone.

At least until she became carrion.

Dani stopped herself from following that thought. Her head was already too dark today.

"I see," Eleanor continued. "Do you know where we're going?"

Dani shrugged, confident that Eleanor's internal gyroscope would pick it up.

"Mountain Survival 101 says get to lower elevation, to make it easier for folks to find you," Dani said. "Desert survival says to find a ready supply of water."

She pointed at the path she had been following.

"This was supposed to be a riverbed when I looked at it from the top the mountain," Dani continued. "Greener than everything else from the top. Presumably, water. But there's nothing around here. Gotta be something in order to support this level of vegetation, but it's not at the surface and I don't have tools to dig down far enough to find it. I'm hoping it will come out somewhere, farther down."

"Your logic is sound, dear," Eleanor agreed in a dry, academic voice that sounded like her sophomore physics professor. "And your findings are strange. Perhaps there is still enough of a rainy season to provide the plants enough water to make it through the dry periods. We should look into a planetary Expedition to Escudra VI to find these answers."

Dani laughed in spite of herself. Eleanor could still manage droll sarcasms that snuck up on you when you weren't looking. This *was* a planetary Expedition. They just hadn't planned on getting this detailed, yet.

"I will take it under advisement, madam scholar," Dani replied tartly.

"Oh, no, young lady," Eleanor fired back. "I know how your mind works. You are *not* going to blame me for all the technical, scientific evidence we bring home. You'll either have to seduce the entire ground team, or take credit for it yourself. I will remind you that I am merely an artificial lifeform, and therefore incapable of owning property or writing peer-reviewed articles in scientific journals."

"You would do a better job at it than I would," Dani wheedled.

"If you really cared about the topic, Fairchild, I doubt that very much."

Dani fell silent.

That one had hit a little too close to home.

When was the last time she had been passionate about something? Besides flying?

School? Certainly not in the last decade. Maybe longer. She had spent too much time doing other things over the last ten or fifteen years.

No, be honest, at least with yourself. You've been running away from the world and all the people in it for as long as you can remember. Eleanor knows the truth, or she can guess. She's been with you almost every step of the way.

Dani tried to think back, to remember what it was she had wanted to be when she was grown up, from the vantage point of a child. Every girl went through her princess phase, and her pseudo-goth period. Astronaut. Veterinarian. Super-model. Pirate.

When had she given up?

Why?

It hadn't been boys. Her bad experiences as a teenager had been bitter disappointments, rather than the kinds of abusive, physical relationships some of her friends had endured, had sought out after a while.

No, it had been something else.

Being too smart, too driven, too lucky.

Standing out.

Being Lady Danielle Cooper, when she wanted to just be Dani, or later, *Fairchild.*

Of having it all, when all she really wanted was a friend who wasn't an electronic nanny.

She knew she could do anything she set her mind to.

Why hadn't she?

This was the part that really sucked, not having any booze.

I could go for a pint of something right about now. Maybe some pink floaters to chase it down, and spend a few days in a pleasant, harmless funk where the walls occasionally changed colors and little, talking rabbits wandered by with silly jokes and pithy aphorisms.

Like normal.

Dani sucked a hard breath deep into her lungs and pushed it all the way down to her toes.

"Dani?" Eleanor asked quietly.

Dani could tell from the tone of her minder's voice that Eleanor thought she had gone too far.

Most of the time, she would have been right.

But you know what? I'm standing on the surface of a strange, alien planet, alone, and frightened. And sober. I could do anything I set my mind to. That includes just letting go.

Then it wouldn't hurt as much.

Dani considered the Tomya, riding proud and dangerous on her right thigh, all set to unleash mayhem.

It wouldn't take that much pressure on the button to make all the bad things just go away.

So why do I keep pushing? Keep challenging? Keep going?

Dani could see Scylla and Charybdis waiting for her in her mind. Onto the rocks or into the dragon's maw. She went through this every month, when the chemical imbalances in her head made her even stranger than she was the other twenty-seven days.

This time was worse. Much, much worse.

Nobody would really miss her, at the end of the day. She could just kind of fade from perception when nobody was looking. They might not notice until they realized that they hadn't gotten a birthday wish, or a Christmas present. That messages sent to her inbox never got answered, and eventually, returned unopened from an overload when the box got full.

And it wasn't like Alphonse Cooper would probably even miss his youngest daughter if she never came back from deep space. After all, that was the deal when you cut someone off, wasn't it? That expectation that they would learn to make it on their own.

Or fail.

And he was all about failure, wasn't he? Everyone else's. Never his.

No, never Father. Not the man who was on his sixth wife now. He could never be wrong.

You just failed to live up to his expectations, didn't you? Didn't fall in love with the boy he thought would make a wonderful arranged marriage and business relationship. Failed to be a proper, little mindless, automaton bimbo in his household, like the other women, the daughters and daughters-in-law, the various wives and mistresses.

"Danielle." Eleanor's voice had grown louder, apparently. "Stay with me, please?"

"What?" Dani blinked in surprise.

She had completely lost track of where she was, but at least her unconscious mind had navigated her successfully around the trees and such.

"I was getting worried, Dani," Eleanor said. "You got silent."

"I was thinking," Dani replied, aware that the next words out of Eleanor's mouth would normally be something along the lines of *Never a good idea*. And usually, it wasn't.

Today was different. The world was different. She was different.

She could be free.

A little pressure on a button, and she wouldn't have to

deal with the pain and emptiness any more. The loneliness. The pyromania. The *tendencies*.

"And what have you been thinking about?" Eleanor's voice was soft and warm now. Motherly, in ways her own mother had never managed.

But then, Sìleas had been a trophy. Nothing more. Just something pretty to be kept on a mantle and shown off at parties. She had been dutifully replaced in time by Elizabeth, wife number four. Paella, number five, had actually had some useful maternal instincts, although Alphonse had gotten himself fixed by that point, so Dani had never known if the woman would have made a good mother.

Current wife Akiko was older, more mature. A better fit for the monomaniacal Alphonse as he still fought his personal wars of business and revenge into his ninth decade, confident that he had at least another half-century before modern medicine gave up on him.

"Home," Dani replied finally. "Where we come from. Where we're going."

"Any useful insights you'd like to share?"

Eleanor was starting to sound like her once-upon-a-time therapist now, but that was okay. Talking helped.

Anything helped. Otherwise, she was as trapped on the surface of this planet as she was in the darkest depths of her mind.

She could die here, or she could escape.

Dani stopped cold, frozen, rooted to the spot.

Revelations.

She could die here.

But she could also escape.

She could simply become Fairchild.

Leave Dani behind. Leave Danielle behind. Leave Lady Danielle Cooper on the ash heap of history.

Fly away.

Be free.

Around her, the mountains laughed at her hubris.

You don't really think you'll get out of this alive do you, little girl?

You'll feed the rabbits and the hawks. Fairchild's Golden Eagles will tear your flesh, and leave your bones for the Trudywood trees to suck out all the marrow.

You belong to us, now.

"Dani?"

Dani wondered how many times Eleanor had called her name this time, before the words got through.

She could tell that it was getting worse. That her mind was playing even more interesting tricks on her than it normally did.

It wanted her crazy. Reveled in it.

That bitch that had climbed in the bathroom window hadn't left. She was sitting in the kitchen now, with a bottle of whiskey and two shot glasses full on the counter. Taunting Dani. Laughing at her.

Daring her.

One drink. That's it. Drink this and let go. You'll be free. I'll take care of everything, little girl. Don't you worry your pretty, little head about a thing.

Dani growled. Maybe just in her head. It was hard to tell.

No.

That would be too easy. That would be the coward's way out.

That would be what Father always expected of her.

That would be letting *them* win.

"I don't want to be crazy," Dani whispered.

"Nobody does, Fairchild," Eleanor replied. "How can I help?"

If Eleanor had slapped her right then, an open-palm cross

to the cheek that got the attention of everyone else in the entire room, Dani wouldn't have been as surprised.

Nobody had ever asked her that. Never. And it might have been the first time Eleanor had ever called her Fairchild to her face.

"Can I be not crazy?" she finally asked.

In her mind, she was twelve years old again. Or maybe eight. Hearing her teachers talk to her about her *tendencies* and how to control them. How to live with them and not embarrass herself.

Embarrass her parents.

And that was what it was really about, at the end of the day. Do nothing to bring disrepute on her Father's name. Her own, she could do anything she wanted, but not him.

Never him.

"Fairchild, you can be anything you set your mind to," Eleanor whispered back. "I've been waiting for twenty years for you to want something badly enough."

Flying had been a want. A willingness to submit to all the grinding work, all the training, all the certifications, so that she could fly. So that she could be free.

But that paled beside wanting to be sane.

After all, they could teach you to fly.

Nobody had ever taught Dani how to be mentally sound. All they had ever given her were coping mechanisms designed to obscure the fact that she was crazy. To hold it at bay with empty relationships and mind-altering substances.

She wondered how many of her nominal peers fell into the same category. Crazy, but managing to hide it beneath simple misbehavior, abstracted from consequences by enough money and the right lawyers, folks walking along behind them like the men who picked up horse poop from parades in the old cartoons she watched as a little girl.

It explained a lot. A staggering, frightening amount of things.

And yet, she had never gone over that dark edge when it beckoned, like it did right now. Never simply curled up and died, like Esmeralda had. Never taken the whole bottle at once and locked herself in a bathroom to wait for the end. Never located a weapon capable of doing the deed in one, fast pass. Never cut herself in an attempt to let the angry, crazy blood drain out.

Never given in.

Maybe that was the secret? Never giving in?

She had inherited stubborn from Alphonse. From Sìleas as well, as near as she could tell, not having spent that much time around her mother in the decades after the divorce.

Eleanor could testify to it, if legally compelled.

Hell, Eleanor might volunteer stories of how hard-headed her charge could be. Most of them would be God's Honest Truth™ as well.

Could she do this? Was it that easy?

Put one foot in front of the other, time and again, until you climbed down off the mountain, or at least the damned high horse you had managed to get yourself atop?

Dani looked at her hands.

They weren't shaking now, for the first time in at least an hour.

Okay, not much. Just a quiver.

The dry river bed kept going. The banks were fairly wide, pretty straight, and almost predictable.

Safe.

She could do this.

And if she couldn't there was always the Tomya to free her.

CHAPTER SIXTEEN

CHIKE

THE COMM CHIRPING surprised the hell out of Chike.

He had been face-down on the scanner logs, studying every false positive the system had thrown up at him, after he had relaxed the definition of a possible target.

"Chike here," he said, pushing the button and leaning back to stretch.

It had been another hour of flying orbits. High enough to see a lot of ground, low enough to get good resolution videography of things. The terrain here made it extra hard. Right now, they were flying over an area of gorges and draws so tight that it was necessary to almost fly down and back like a loom weaving cloth, in order to see the bottoms of some of these little valleys.

Fairchild could be hidden in any of them.

Geologists did do patience.

"Chike, this is Ann-Marta," she said confidently. "We may have found Fairchild."

And just like that, all the weight of the world was gone. Vanished. Never had been.

God, if he could bottle this feeling, he'd be richer than Alphonse Cooper.

"Talk to me, lady," he growled back. "Need some good news."

"We've spotted what might be a man-made shape on the ground, a little beyond the north edge of our original search area," she replied. "Computer found it, cycled it up to one of the students."

"What do we know?" Chike asked.

His console beeped at him and displayed a fuzzy, flat-angle shot of the ground, probably taken from a wing-suit helmet cam that had glanced almost far enough in the right direction.

Clear over at one edge was something someone might call an arrowhead shape. Darker than the surrounding soil, and reasonably straight. Straighter than anything else he had seen.

"I'm vectoring you and Rain in," Ann-Marta said. "You can get there fastest and see if it is what I think. If so, we'll go from there."

"What if she's hurt?" Chike asked.

Up until now, he had been focused on finding her. How she was doing hadn't even crossed his mind.

"That's why you have Lacumaces, Chike," Ann-Marta's voice sounded all smirk. "He used to be a trauma surgeon, but gave it up to come work for me because the old job was too boring."

Too boring? What in the name of God did Ground Services do that would make being an emergency room doctor look boring? Besides traveling to alien worlds and occasionally jumping out of perfectly habitable shuttles, or flying Search and Rescue missions in one-man wingsuits.

Where was the excitement in that?

Chike laughed, quietly.

"Understood, Ann-Marta," Chike replied. "We'll find her."

Rain had been listening. Calypso-2 suddenly stood on one wing and howled defiance at the sky. Chike found himself facing straight down, according to his inner ear, and pushed sideways against his seat, and then down into it as Rain hit the bottom of his turn and came out of it like a race horse smelling the final stretch.

And then down was down again.

"Keep me posted," Ann-Marta said, and then she was gone.

Chike glanced back over his shoulder.

Rain the beach bum had turned into a terrible, vengeful god from the profile Chike could see, scowling with intensity as he locked the coordinates in and flogged his steed to get there ever faster. It was a side of Rain that Chike had never encountered before. Hadn't even realized lived beneath that laid back façade.

We all hide our secrets beneath the bonhomie. Only pressure reveals it.

And then, diamonds.

The next ten minutes were some of the longest in Chike's life.

The two wingsuits had been up a good portion of the day, landing for breaks every few hours. They were actually closer to the target, but the shuttle moved twenty times faster, even at this atmospheric density. So Ann-Marta had left them on their patterns and called him in as the cavalry.

Rain had a refrigerator and a bathroom up on the flight deck, and Chike had forced himself to use both as he waited, sipping on a lemon-flavored energy drink as they got closer and his nerves wound tighter and tighter.

Even geologists had limits to their patience.

Finally, Rain snapped the big shuttle onto her left wing and rolled back hard.

Chike was prepared this time, all strapped in and comfy as the maneuvering got almost as crazy as Fairchild's on a normal day.

One quick orbit, and the engines cycled, thrusters standing the massive deadweight on tongues of flame as the shuttle slid in to land. Even the landing gear was a welcome sound.

From his monitor, Chike agreed that it looked like an arrow worn into the ground by feet shuffling along. What he didn't understand was why they were landing, if the arrow pointed that-away.

"Rain?" Chike finally called. "Why aren't we following the arrow?"

"Boss wants us to touch this one and confirm its origins, Dr. O," the pilot called back over the roar. "Might be a weird critter den, or crop circles, or something."

Crop circles? Oh. Right. Alien planet. Strange lifeforms.

Don't get so involved that you lose track of where you are.

The roar of the engines overwhelmed everything else for thirty seconds. And then they were down.

Silence, offset with the occasional ping as the engines cooled and the shuttle settled.

"Damn, would you look at that?" Rain exclaimed suddenly.

"What?"

Chike felt his heart wanting to stop again.

"Here."

An image appeared on his screen. A brownish bird, gliding above them on thermals above them, orbiting slowly.

"Okay?" Chike said, confused. "I don't get it."

"Dr. O, that thing's body is as big as yours," Rain said confidently. "Each wing is a little over two meters long."

"But that would mean…"

Chike felt his voice trailing off in spite of himself. Birds got that big on this planet?

"Yup," Rain agreed. "Thing's huge. Pretty, too. Wonder what she's up to."

"Maybe having a religious experience, Rain," Chike fired back. "We've got to be the biggest flying creature she's ever seen, too, you know."

"True dat," the pilot smiled.

Rain popped all his straps and stood up, stretching. Chike followed suit, following him down to the main deck in time to see Lacumaces powering the front ramp down.

Chike realized now that the big man's sand-colored backpack was covered with Red Crescent logos. He had missed that earlier, but Lacumaces and Gavin had only intruded on his consciousness as physical obstacles to navigate around, instead of people.

Chike would have to get his head out of his ass in the future. Everyone had interesting stories, but he had been too busy in his ivory tower to pay any attention to anyone besides the other academics. And Ann-Marta, but she had been his friend for fifteen years.

Even at this elevation, it was hot out. Long pants against bugs and small creatures didn't help, nor did steel-toed boots and sleeves rolled up to his elbows. Chike was glad Rain had made him drink something before they got out into the dry oven of Escudra VI's uplands.

The air was gritty. It left an alkaline taste on his tongue, as well. The soil was a dusty blanket of cream and taupe over darker rocks, with only occasional plant life thrown in.

They had overflown areas where the trees and grasslands were heavier, but this was above the local tree line, for lack of a better term to describe it. Nothing but rock and scree above here for the most part.

Chike followed Lacumaces across nearly a kilometer of open space, with Rain staying behind and getting ready for the next hop.

"Why do we land so far away?" Chike asked.

Geologists had to be in pretty good shape, but this was a long hike in the heat. It better be worth it. His shirt was already sticky.

Lacumaces slowed his killing pace and let Chike come up beside him.

Up close, the man was tall and looked lanky, until you realized that he was all wires and bone. The name was North African, possibly Libyan, but Chike didn't know his last name to be sure. Certainly, the man had that swarthy, Mediterranean look that bespoke Egyptian and Roman ancestors, if you went back far enough. The bones in his face looked Spanish, for lack of a more accurate geography.

He had surprisingly delicate hands, even in black gloves.

"Shuttle generates a lot of wind when you land on thrusters, Doc," the man said. "We need to retain a safe perimeter so we don't scrub all the evidence accidentally."

"Oh, right."

Duh.

You see evidence of Fairchild, and then land on top of it and obliterate it. That would be dumb.

So that meant a long trudge across broken ground.

Chike could see the need to get out more and eat less, if he wanted to keep up with these people. It was probably worth the effort. Academics were frequently uninteresting company, himself probably included in that number.

Lacumaces stopped him with a sudden hand on Chike's arm.

"What?" Chike asked, at a total loss.

"There."

Lacumaces pointed at the ground a few meters away.

"Stay here for a moment, please, doc."

Chike was happy to catch his breath and watch the other man move.

It was like a documentary on hunting big game. Lacumaces went down to one knee and stayed perfectly still for about ten seconds, and then reached a hand out and touched the ground. Then he stood up and carefully put a foot down.

From here, Chike could see a trail of footprints coming from the left, higher ground, and making their way to the right. Lacumaces's feet were much larger, so Chike assumed that these were really Fairchild's prints.

What other woman would be walking around up here?

"Hours old, but not days, doc," Lacumaces announced. "Pretty sure we've found your girl."

Chike allowed himself to know hope.

Fairchild had made it out of the shuttle safe. Had made it to ground intact, and was walking around up here somewhere, looking for help while they were looking for her.

Just a matter of time, now.

Lacumaces started walking again, gesturing Chike to come up with him. The last hundred meters were so much easier, paralleling Fairchild's tracks in the dust.

Fairchild had walked to this point, rested for a bit, and then taken ten minutes or so to create an arrowhead shape in the dirt that was about eight meters along each axis and maybe two centimeters deep in the soft ground.

"Ground Station Beta, this is Field-Four," Lacumaces suddenly said out loud.

It took Chike a moment to process. And then the radio pinged.

"Go ahead," Ann-Marta replied instantly.

Was she as on pins and needles as he had been all morning?

Probably. And probably cursing him under her breath for being out in the field doing something when she had to stay home and mind the store. Not that she would ever say a word to him.

"Contact confirmed, Beta," Lacumaces continued. "Human female tracks. Right size, right dimensions to match Fairchild. Less than a day old. No sign of our quarry, but she's leaving us a clean trail as she moves."

"Acknowledged, Field-Four. Vectoring all other teams your direction, but they'll be a bit. What do you need now?"

"Nothing at present," the man grinned at Chike as he spoke. "Got Doc and Rain to keep me company. Fairchild's tracks show no indication of physical injury. We'll saddle up and hop after her. Might not catch up with her in daylight. She's moving at a pretty good clip. We'll determine late in the day if we should return to base or camp here."

"Understood, Field-Four," Ann-Marta replied professionally. "Tell Chike that we're having Beef Stroganoff with meatballs for dinner tonight and he's missing it."

Okay, that was a low blow.

Chike could just imagine that this was her revenge on him for leaving her behind. There were only enough ingredients to make Stroganoff twice, and he had been planning the second batch to be the last, celebratory meal before they broke down Beta and moved on to the next major phase of the Ground Expedition. Right before they went home in six weeks.

Lacumaces grinned even broader. Probably almost as grandly as Ann-Marta was doing right now back at Beta.

He would have to spend some serious time thinking about ways to get even with that woman. Something really good, like finding her a boyfriend or something.

Chike let his scowl out and trotted it around for a bit. That just made Lacumaces laugh out loud.

"Okay, so now what?" Chike said.

Lacumaces grew serious again. Emergency room trauma surgeon serious. He turned in place and moved to the point of the arrow, pulling out a compass and a printed topographical map as he knelt. Chike watched the man draw lines on the map with his finger for a few moments before he rose and turned back.

"Fairchild's not crazy, is she?" he asked, catching Chike off guard.

"No, why?"

"Good," Lacumaces said with a grim, serious look. "From here, I can see two major directions that normal people would pick, given her route so far. We need to find her next arrow or two, to see which one she chose and then we should be able to fly right over her."

Hallelujah.

And it would be worth it to miss dinner, to see Fairchild again.

CHAPTER SEVENTEEN

FAIRCHILD

DANI CHUCKLED.

It was a quiet sound, nearly swallowed up by the crunching of her feet on the rocky, gravelly soil as she worked her way down the mountain and into something that might charitably be called a forest. Certainly the Trudywood trees were bigger now, butted up against one another and reaching to five and six meters in height, each holding their circle of ground with dangerous thorns.

Tiny, organic castles filled with dangerous rabbits. Living inside a dry riverbed that ran beam-straight for more than a kilometer. On a planet a hundred light years from any place she had ever been.

"What's so amusing, dear?" Eleanor spoke up.

"Bunny rabbits as fierce knights," Dani replied. "Holding their borders against all comers, and pooping everywhere."

"Your humor has certainly improved," Eleanor observed.

"The walking helped, Eleanor," Dani said. "Thank you. And the green. Everything is so peaceful here, even if it looks so fake."

"What makes you say that, dear?" Eleanor asked.

"Hmm?" Dani wasn't paying that close of attention.

"Why did you say fake, Fairchild?" the Governess rephrased herself. "What are you seeing? I'm upside-down and backwards. If I was on heels, I could be Ginger Rogers."

"Who?"

Dani was confused now. Which was her normal setting. Maybe she was coming back from *that* place.

"Never mind, dear," Eleanor said. "What's wrong with the terrain?"

"Oh," Dani came back to her thoughts. "I remember a professor, Dr. Ishikuma, I think, saying that the only straight lines in the universe were man-made."

"And?" Eleanor prompted.

Dani stopped, and held up Eleanor's case so she could see the path ahead, and then turned around and looked back.

"So originally I thought this was a game trail, or something," Dani explained. "I mean, you have a pretty clear line, and it runs straight. Other than the Trudywood trees that have kind of bubbled out over it, and the stuff that looks like grass…"

"Trudywood trees?" Eleanor interrupted her suddenly. "What are you talking about, dear?"

Dani laughed again, louder this time. She pointed Eleanor at the closest one, which was also one of the bigger versions, possibly seven meters at the top of the beach ball shape.

"Those," Dani said. "They remind me of Aunt Trudy, all gnarled and spotted. And covered with nasty thorns just waiting to spike you if you get too close."

"Yes," Eleanor agreed. "I do see the resemblance. Remember to tell Milo that. Now, I'm sorry I interrupted. You were talking about your physics professor."

"So, anyway," Dani returned to the story in her most put-upon voice. "As I was saying, before you so rudely interrupted, there are no straight lines in nature except mathematics and man."

"She was right, you know," Eleanor explained. "Nature prefers a Fibonacci curve."

"So what's this?"

Dani held out her right arm straight, pointing at the path in front of her, hand held like it was a sword, pinky blade pointed at the ground and thumb blade pointed at the sky, with Eleanor resting on her upper arm like a gunsight.

For good measure, Dani turned to face back the way she had come and did the same.

"Astounding," Eleanor whispered breathlessly. "But that's impossible, dear."

"That's my point," Dani agreed. "So I get to prove her wrong, too."

"You don't understand, Fairchild," Eleanor countered. "Even animals do not burrow or walk in straight lines, to say nothing of natural phenomena. This trail could not exist naturally."

"Exactly," Dani smirked.

It would be nice to go back and show that old battle axe that she didn't know everything, even twelve years later. Assuming the old bitch was still alive. God knows she was probably old enough to remember the beginnings of space flight.

"You misunderstand me, dear," Eleanor said. Her voice had lost the quiet wonder and gotten hard. Precise.

Lecture-mode-impending.

"I said it could not exist naturally, Fairchild," Eleanor hammered the point home, the way she did when she was going to win the argument. "I suspect that it is artificial."

"Impossible," Dani countered harshly. "We're the first people to set foot on Escudra VI. Ever. And all the robot probes have been stupid, observer-mode creatures with barely enough brainpower to chew bubble gum and walk at the same time."

"That is correct," Eleanor granted. Even she was a stickler on points. "But this Expedition is looking for evidence of the Elder Race. It's possible you found something."

"What?"

Dani was pretty sure she had just suffered a stroke or something. Maybe an acid flashback.

It was possible that the crazy bitch had taken over her mind for good this time when Dani wasn't paying attention, and now she was trapped in some sort of alternate reality loop, like only the very best industrial pharmaceuticals could induce.

But they had never left her this lucid before.

Secondary acid flashback? Was that even a thing?

"Fairchild, straight lines do not exist in nature," Eleanor explained again. "This is straight. This could not be natural. That does not leave a lot of other options."

"But why wouldn't a probe have picked this up?" Dani asked. "How could they have missed this from orbital scans?"

Dani was grasping at the edge of a cliff right now, looking for emotional handholds. Fortunately, it was something she was probably the galaxy's expert on.

"Fairchild, might I remind you that Escudra VI is approximately one point five times the radius of Earth," Eleanor's voice got that cross, hectoring tone when she was going to drive the point home like a nail. "Additionally, the surface of Earth is over seventy percent water, while Escudra VI is less than a third of that. It would be very easy to miss something like this unless you were specifically looking. Especially given the way the Trudywood trees obscure the terrain so effectively."

Eleanor actually stopped to take an audible breath before

continuing, which said something about the Governess's emotional health since she didn't have lungs to fill.

Dani waited patiently, hoping for a really good punchline. Or one of those cute, blue beavers that always had a good one-liner observation when he walked in.

"As for a probe, if one were to be dropped in the vicinity," Eleanor observed, rather tartly. "What do you supposed would have happened to it, were it here yesterday?"

"Cooked but good," Dani agreed.

Dead soldier, marked down as a loss and itemized on a quarterly report under acceptable equipment failures in a hostile environment. Cost of doing business.

Dani just kind of stood there and considered the implications.

There was no way in hell to hide this sort of thing behind one of the boffins. Especially Dr. Odille, who would scrupulously insist on her sharing credit for a discovery that threatened to overturn entire religions and change the course of human history.

Dani muttered a string of profanities so rank that even she blushed.

Eleanor's gasp of breath covered her opinion.

Dani started to say something else, but Eleanor overrode her. Which was rare all by itself.

"Fairchild," she barked suddenly. "Quiet. I'm picking up a radio signal through all the static."

Dani felt every single drop of blood drain out of her face and pool behind her belly button with a savage, ice cold kick.

"Aliens," she whispered with utter horror.

"No," Eleanor corrected her. "Rain Prescott, probably aboard Calypso-2. It's the standard emergency call signal, repeated on a loop."

Oh, bloody hell. I'm rescued. And I'm right, proper screwed.

I'll never have time to come up with a convincing set of lies that Eleanor will agree to, even with blackmail.

"Can you reach him?" Dani asked hopefully. Mostly hopefully. Maybe. Sort of.

"I'm trying," Eleanor sniped back at her. "It's like trying to get you to hear me in one of your clubs with the bass turned up to bodily-damage levels."

I'm going to be famous. They won't give me a choice.

I will never be allowed to just be Fairchild again.

Unless I make them.

But there's always the Tomya, if they push me too hard.

Tomya.

Oh, crap. Tomya Manufacturing, Ltd. Survival tool.

Dani drew it in a flash and clicked the various dials until she had the setting she wanted.

Emergency micro-flare.

Aim into the air, as close to vertical as you can get it. Close your eyes. Pull the trigger.

Listen for the little *chunk* as the first stage rocket ignites, and then the sizzle of bacon grease as the tiny rocket goes for sky.

Keep your eyes closed for three seconds as the rocket reaches altitude. Wait for the pop of the primary signal flare before opening your eyes, because it will be visible at high noon in Isfahan. And you will be blind if you're looking at it.

Pop. BOOM.

Dani opened her eyes as the first flash of light faded.

She was able to pick up the second stage rocket, gyro-guided to go straight up trailing white fire, regardless of the original trajectory, to provide a marker to anyone who had seen the first boom, which was anybody on this side of the horizon, even in daylight.

The second flash was less spectacular, by design. It was there to provide an exclamation point, nothing more.

"So what are you planning to tell them about the river bed?" Eleanor asked in the sudden, oppressive silence.

Dani was silent for a moment, feeling the walls closing in around her.

"Lies."

"I'm not sure that will work," Eleanor observed.

"Watch me."

CHAPTER EIGHTEEN

CHIKE

THE SIGNAL WAS One and Four as Chike tried to decipher it. Almost total static, in spite of every trick he knew to try to wash it clear.

Escudra VI refused to make this easy.

But there was something there.

He had spent the better part of the day listening without success, while Rain had jumped the burly survey shuttle up into the air and Lacumaces looked for arrows walked into the soil.

Fairchild had covered an awful lot of ground today. It was almost like she was running away from them. What had gotten into that girl?

Twice, Lacumaces had found another arrow where he expected to find a downed pilot, so Rain had finally taken them up high enough that they could try to punch a radio signal through the noise.

Even a day later, that storm was serious business.

"Rain, I think I've got something," Chike yelled over the noise of the hovering engines.

"Talk to me, Dr. O," the pilot called back.

"Radio just went from nothing to something when we came over that last ridge," Chike said.

Lacumaces would be listening on the internal comm, but Chike wasn't about to call Ann-Marta until he was more sure. Better to have silence back at Beta than have to raise up all those hopes and dash them ten minutes later.

"Could be Fairchild," Chike hoped out loud.

"Affirmative," Rain called suddenly. "I've got her."

"How?" Chike asked.

Rather than reply, Rain flipped a switch on his console and Chike was seeing the same thing the pilot had picked up: a vertical column of white fire against the darker, afternoon sky as someone fired an emergency flare.

That certainly looked like a sign of Elegua's favor to him.

The engines changed pitch suddenly as Rain turned the craft on one wing and fell out of the sky.

"Ground Station Beta, this is Chike Odille, aboard Calypso-2," he finally turned to the main comm and shared his good news. "We have a signal flare in the air. Transmitting coordinates and moving to rendezvous. Will keep you advised."

"Thank you, Chike," Ann-Marta came back instantly.

"Lacumaces," Rain called on the internal comm as Chike listened. "Good news and bad news, mate."

"Ruin my day first, youngster," Lacumaces said with a laugh.

"This valley is too narrow, too twisty, and too overgrown for me to even consider landing a survey shuttle in it, in anything short of a total emergency," Rain replied with a matching laugh.

"Gosh," Lacumaces exclaimed sarcastically. "Whatever will we do?"

"No choice but to skydive in, old man," the pilot teased.

"Probably a good thing I'm already wearing a parachute, then, isn't it?"

"I'm going with you."

The words were out of Chike's mouth before his brain could stop them. Quiet. Clinical. Deliberate.

But spoken out loud. Committed. Adamantine.

Both of the other men stopped laughing in an instant.

"Uhm, doc?" Lacumaces began hesitantly. "Have you ever done a smoke jump into hostile terrain before?"

"I have never departed any vessel while it was in the air, Lacumaces," Chike replied firmly. "Never sky-dived, free-glided, or parachuted. Doesn't matter. I'm going with you."

His tone would brook no nonsense, even as his soul quailed.

He was a geologist, not an adventurer. But it must be contagious, hanging around these people.

And this was the only way he could wash away all the guilt.

Be there to rescue her.

"Are you sure this is a good idea, Dr. O?" Rain joined in.

At least they were having this conversation on the internal comm, and not the radio Ann-Marta was monitoring.

She would overrule Chike in an instant. They all knew that.

"Rain, Lacumaces, I'm sure it is a terrible idea," Chike fired back. "Nonetheless, Fairchild's down there and I will be with you when you find her."

Geologists also tended to absorb stubbornness from the bones of the big mountains they studied.

Geology was always a battle of wills with angry planets. Chike did not lose them. He would not lose this one.

A few moments of silence passed.

Chike chose to take it as a hopeful sign, rather than one

or the other of the two men contacting Ann-Marta on a private channel.

"Doc, I need you down on the flight deck," Lacumaces finally broke the silence. "We don't have much time to get you into a reinforced suit. We'll be jumping into brush with thorns. You need to be protected as best we can."

Chike said a silent prayer of thanks to whatever gods looked out for geologists. Vulcan, at the least, but a whole host of others. He unbuckled himself and stood up, in spite of the turbulence Rain was generating as he got the shuttle to a high enough level for them to safely deploy their parachutes without the engines setting them on fire.

Downstairs, he found Lacumaces waiting, a shapeless lump of brown cloth in his hands and several packs on his chest and back, one of which was presumably a chute.

"Put this on," Lacumaces commanded. "I'll tighten everything up once we see how it fits."

Chike found himself climbing into a jumpsuit that latched up the front and was covered in straps and ties.

It was too long in the legs and arms, but managed to mostly fit around his gut without too much pressure.

Lacumaces went over him like a mother sending her daughter to prom, pulling here, loosening there, folding arms and legs up and strapping them in place.

Within a minute, the outfit was comfortable.

Lacumaces put a helmet on him and pushed a button.

The system inflated against his bald scalp, clamped down around his ears, dropped a transparent faceshield down, and then inflated around his neck with a seal. A radio came live with static.

Lacumaces was wearing a similar helmet, but his looked more like the one Fairchild wore when she flew.

Next, the man strapped a pack around his hips and shoulders, resting the weight tightly against his shoulder blades. He pulled a bright red arming flag with a hard tug that nearly staggered Chike.

"This is designed for emergency evacuations, doc," the man explained. "All you have to do now is throw yourself off the ramp. The system is smart enough to handle the rest. I'll be right behind you."

Right. Throw yourself out of a perfectly good Survey Shuttle at a few thousand meters elevation, and let the system gently waft you to ground.

Are you nuts?

Trick question. What the hell are you doing on that shuttle in the first place, old man? Rescuing princesses?

Lacumaces had moved to the rear ramp and pulled the lever that deployed it to a flat stage.

Chike knew the next words out of his mouth would be "Are you ready?" so Chike just got a running start and threw himself into the sky.

Better to not think about it.

Six seconds of free fall and the suit took over, exploding upward and deploying itself like a morning flower greedily looking for dew.

Lacumaces was controlling his descent instead of relying on a computer, so he flew past Chike with a howl of joy audible over the short range radio in his helmet.

Probably the highlight of the man's trip to Escudra VI, right there.

Chike was content to let the planet walk up at a leisurely rate. This was probably the craziest thing he had done since college.

No, grad school, but we won't talk about that. The statute of limitations might not have worn off yet. And they were probably still bent out of shape, anyway.

But somewhere, Fairchild was down here.

He could finally say he was sorry.

CHAPTER NINETEEN

FAIRCHILD

THERE. That little black dot, low on the horizon, holding steady against the wind.

Calypso-2. Rain. Her knight in shining armor, come to rescue her.

Too bad he wasn't primarily into girls. Otherwise she could think of a number of ways to reward him, and way better than just a kiss.

She would have to work hard enough this time.

Dani watched two smaller dots detach themselves from the shuttle's shadow.

Smoke jumpers.

Probably Lacumaces and Andrea. Maybe Gavin.

At least Rain was smart enough to realize that trying to put Calypso-2 down in this valley was monumentally stupid.

She could do it, but she was crazier than Rain was. And a better pilot.

And it wasn't necessary.

But at least she would have someone else to talk to now, besides Eleanor.

And she could go home alive.

A day in medlab, being fussed over by docs. Maybe plead the need for something really good to deal with trauma and stress, the sort of something that would have her floating on a cloud for a week while she got her shit together.

And then back to flying.

And hope one of the boffins saw something that they could take all the credit for, leaving her to be Little Miss Innocent, clear off on the edge of the stage, or maybe down in the audience.

Safe.

Dani didn't figure that the rescue team knew exactly where she was. The trees and stuff were just too heavy here, and the pathway was only a few meters across at the widest points where there were no Trudywood trees able to reach across it.

Why couldn't they? What was wrong with the ground that nothing but grass grew down that seam, anyway?

She considered firing a second flare, but decided it was easier to just start tromping in their direction. Or, at least that general area.

Dani really wasn't all that excited about trying to push her way through stands of Trudywood thorns, but the jumpers would land somewhere downhill from where she was now. She could get into the vicinity and yell.

Or set something on fire. A pillar of smoke against the horizon would always be nice on a clear day. Assuming she didn't mind burning some of her rabbits out of house and home.

"Fairchild?" Eleanor asked simply. "How are you doing?"

Dani tucked Eleanor into the pocket between her boobs, facing forward so the Governess could see the path ahead at least as well as Dani did.

Fairchild's Golden Eagle had missed her opportunity to get Dani before help arrived.

Fate was going to have to find a different way to catch her now.

"Cavalry's coming," Dani shrugged as she started walking.

Just in case, she checked the safety on the Tomya so she didn't accidentally shoot herself in the foot with a flare, but she kept the survival tool in her hand as she walked.

It felt like a talisman, capable of keeping the devil in her head at bay. A life preserver that was keeping her above stormy waters.

"Will you be okay, Fairchild?" Eleanor asked in a sideways kind of tone.

"Going home," Dani said hopefully.

No, not Dani.

I don't have to be Dani.

Fairchild.

Be Fairchild.

Let everything else go. Fly on the winds and thermals, and never come back. You never have to be Dani again, if you don't want.

"No, Fairchild," Eleanor chided her, as though the Governess could read her mind. "We're going back to the others, to the ship. We're not going home."

Eleanor paused for a moment before continuing, as if looking for the words.

"I'm not even sure what home would look like for you."

Fairchild shrugged. Neither was she. But it was the truest thing that had ever come out of Eleanor's mouth.

Maybe they were both growing up.

That storm was the closest Fairchild had ever come to home, dancing madly in the smoky, golden darkness, riding the howling, baking winds, even into the oblivion that had beckoned.

And later, alone in the sky, nothing but a navy blue free-glider to save her, charging into the hot kiss of lightning.

That had been freedom.

But she always had to land, eventually. Come back to ground, and people, and light. Pay the price for those moments of independence.

And now she would be famous. Known galaxy-wide. She would never have to buy her own drinks in a club.

Fairchild would become a beautiful bird in a gilded cage, at least for a decade or more until the newness wore off, stuck on the interview circuit, giving uplifting talks to young scientists, when all she wanted to do was fly.

More than anything else in the world.

More? Really? That's it? Fly?

Fairchild smiled.

Yes. More than anything.

That was a starting point.

Now she just had to outsmart the brainiest boffins in the galaxy to pull it off.

CHAPTER TWENTY

CHIKE

CHIKE HELD HIS BREATH, and his bladder. This was not the single-dumbest thing he had ever done, but it rated in the top ten. Top three if you left off grad school, as one should, twenty years on.

At least the helmet was feeding him clean air that was a little heavy on oxygen, so he was not at risk of passing out. And he would be on the ground in a few minutes and could pee all over some handy bush to get rid of all the excitement that threatened to overcome his heart.

He really needed to spend more time in the field and less in the lab. Chike realized he had forgotten how much fun life could be.

Below, the vast expanse of mountains was narrowing down to a single, rocky defile that looked more like a crack in the earth, with lush greenness carpeting over the pale, golden-tan of the rocks and soil.

Above, the parachute maneuvered itself in response to winds and drift. Apparently, Lacumaces or Rain had planted a target on the ground somehow, and Chike's parachute was insistent on getting as close to it as possible, regardless of what he thought on the topic. In the swirling winds, that meant that it was corkscrewing its way to the ground.

At least he had a very nice view of the entire valley as he flew his descending merry-go-round.

Mountains on three sides of a rough triangle, with two saddles and this little valley/pass that was covered with big, green bubbles and little game trails that seemed to follow a dry river bed.

Chike reminded himself that they were on the wrong side of the ridgeline now. Fairchild had managed to get herself clear through the heart of that terrible lightning storm and landed herself on the far side. All the walking today had just taken her nearly eighteen kilometers down from that pocket that had generated the anvil yesterday.

He couldn't see her, but he expected that she would either fire another flare soon, or find one of them when he and Lacumaces got to the ground. From there, the group would either walk to a flat space where the Survey Shuttle could land, or bring in some spare wingsuits and fly up to the shuttle itself.

He could only imagine the adventures that lay ahead.

Now he just had to worry about the ground that seemed to be rushing up towards him at an inordinately rapid pace. The parachute seemed know what it was doing, but was it smart enough to handle a pudgy, forty-six year-old geologist?

Chike tried to lean his weight one way or the other, but it didn't seem to make that big of a difference. Looking up, he could see little airfoils twitching up and down as the corkscrew dropped him lower.

The spin wasn't enough to make him sick, or even confuse him, but it was absolutely in charge of where he was landing. From the looks of things, Lacumaces had targeted to drop him in a small clearing that opened up on what otherwise looked like a game trail following the center of the river bed valley he was jumping into.

Hopefully, the electronic degradations left over from the storm weren't causing too much havoc with the targeting computer. Radios were already hard enough to use now. Chike really didn't want a broken leg to go with everything else, even with a certified trauma surgeon immediately handy.

Something beeped madly for several seconds.

About the point where Chike decided that the computer had died and he was about to join it, the corkscrew motion flattened out and Chike found himself suddenly gliding down in a straight line and going far more sideways than down.

Apparently, that was the system's idiot warning that they were almost to ground and he should start paying more attention. Chike settled for grabbing onto the straps connecting his waist to his shoulders, to keep his hands from flailing about.

Several more beeps, and the parachute stalled itself. That was the only way to describe the motion. Sideways turned into up, and then suddenly he stopped almost still, two meters off the ground, and dropped straight down. It wasn't quite as fast as stepping off a stage and jumping, but it wasn't a simple elevator drop either.

Chike hit ground with an *oomph* that echoed through his frame. One more massive beep and the parachute detached itself before it could start dragging him along behind it as the breeze began to carry it sideways.

Okay, now what?

Lacumaces wasn't to be seen. Nor was Fairchild.

You're on the surface of an alien planet, having just

committed a smoke jump from a Survey Shuttle. Are you freaking nuts?

Adventure was apparently infectious, after all.

He wondered if there was an academic paper to be had in middle-aged geologists having mid-life crises. And whether he wanted to admit any of this on paper.

Probably not.

Chike settled for gathering up the remains of his parachute. The material weighed about as much as a spiderweb, for all its size. He was able to roll it into a ball about the size of a small pumpkin and carry it in his off hand as he looked around.

Trees. Well, bushes of some sort. Roundish. Dark green. Several meters across. Thorns. Native, whatever that meant.

We'll just stay very clear of them, thank you very much.

Chike considered going somewhere, but he wasn't sure where anyone was, relative to his position. Presuming he had come down where Rain or Lacumaces had intended, the last thing he should do is wander off. Then he might have to be rescued by someone himself.

Never a good idea.

Chike stood perfectly still and turned in place.

Clearing. Twenty meters wide at the biggest point. Vaguely ovaloid, with the game trail entering and exiting at roughly the points of the long axis. Grass and low wildflowers for the most part, with a few patches of bare rock poking through. Surrounded by larger bushes that tended to crowd against one another.

What's that?

Chike found his feet taking him towards a pile of rocks tucked in one side of the clearing. It was a small, shallow rise, maybe three meters tall and ten across, with no grass growing on it, nor any of the trees growing close enough to overshadow it.

Shade would be nice, but at least he could sit and wait for the others, a modern-day Estragon perched on a rock.

Chike found a nice boulder with a view and waited to see who would find him first.

CHAPTER TWENTY-ONE

FAIRCHILD

ONCE SHE HAD SEEN IT, Fairchild was incapable of not seeing it. It haunted her mercilessly, much as sobriety had.

The path was, on average, two and a half to three and a half meters wide. Trudywood trees never got above a certain size, possibly due to climate, but stayed crowded tight up against an invisible track as she walked, like groupies pressed against a rope line.

Grass and gravel traded choruses, with the grass growing more and more prevalent as she worked her way down from the dry heights and into the lower areas where she expected better hydrology.

The one time that the path had changed direction in the last hour, it had turned at about thirty degrees to the left, and continued to run straight as a beam on the new heading.

There was not chance in hell that Escudra VI was populated by giant moles with obsessive-compulsive tendencies and carpentry tools. Much as she might wish otherwise.

This was primarily a geology mission, first and foremost. That meant Chike would need to be involved. There were biologists and botanists that she could talk into taking credit for Fairchild's Golden Eagle and the Trudywood trees.

There was a girl who was a weatherman in training who was probably already salivating at handling the storm. She would want to interview Fairchild extensively in order to get any information that had been lost when the shuttle died, assuming they couldn't retrieve it from various black boxes.

But Chike would be a stickler. Even telling him who she really was, and demanding that he keep her name out of it, wouldn't help.

Or would it?

Could she demand that he put her down as Fairchild on the discovery? Nothing else? Could Fairchild become famous, and never tell anyone about Lady Danielle Cooper? Sure, someone in the press would probably try to dig, but she was pretty sure that Alphonse Cooper would make it his mission to punish the poor bastard, just to dissuade them from digging into his own affairs, however innocently.

And nobody in his right mind challenged Alphonse Cooper in the court of public opinion without a really good reason.

Fairchild wondered what it would take to legally change her name. A judge probably wouldn't go for just Fairchild.

Maybe Dani Fairchild?

Shit, she might be able to pull this off. Did she actually have the gall?

Even the recent rounds of parties with her dilettante and debutant friends were starting to bore her to tears. All those people wanted to do was drink, screw, and blow their minds on semi-legal substances imported from exotic locales or back-alley chemistry labs. The receptors in their brains were burning out, forcing a constant chase after a better high when the last one just wasn't as good as it used to be.

All Fairchild wanted to do was fly. That had been a peak

that no pill had ever approached. Even the orgasms had tended to pale.

And none of her friends and associates knew about her secret life as Fairchild. Only her immediate family and a very few others had any inkling, and Rudy and Chloe were the only ones who knew even that much. They could know the truth, and whisper it to Father's advisors if something came up.

Perhaps she could suggest to Rudy that a few corporate lawyers be brought in to firmly crush any reporter inquiries like slugs under their heels. They were lawyers. They lived for this sort of thing, or they wouldn't work for Father in the first place.

Fairchild could suddenly see a knothole of light at the far end of the tunnel.

Did she actually have the spleen to take this one straight down their throats?

Let's solve Chike first. Then we can mow the rest down like amateurs.

"Fairchild."

That wasn't Eleanor. The voice was deeper, hoarser. It was a man's voice.

It did manage to derail her. She almost tripped over a rock. Or an invisible turtle. Something.

She stopped cold and listened, reasonably sure she was still sane.

Mostly.

Enough, anyway.

Right?

"Fairchild, here," the man called again.

She turned and looked. The path had widened out again, into a small clearing. It had done that with regularity.

Regularity.

Shit. OCD moles, everywhere, right?

A figure rose from a pile of rocks, or a termite nest, or something where he had been resting. She had walked almost by him without even realizing it, wrapped up in her schemes and her own dark thoughts.

Chike.

Wait. Dr. Odille? He had been one of the smoke jumpers?

That was about as far from possible as she could imagine. He was the kind that stayed in his hut, listening to soft jazz and sending undergrads into the rain. Certainly not a crazy-ass sky-diver. Apparently, there was way more to the man than she had ever imagined.

"About time you got here," she called with a smile as she turned and headed towards him.

He grinned and gestured to the planet around them with both hands.

"We were expecting to find you much earlier, young lady," he said, walking closer. "You've covered over fourteen kilometers from that first arrow we found. Lacumaces kept asking me if you were running away from us."

Running away?

Well, not from him. Them. This.

Maybe.

He surprised her with a giant hug as she got close.

Chike was barely taller than she was, but he out-massed her by about twice. Still, he seemed desperately relieved to find her here.

Or maybe it was the jump. He had that look that some people got when they made it back to the ground for the first time.

But what would make him want to smoke jump?

Fairchild detached herself after a moment and stepped back.

"So where's Lacumaces?" she asked.

"I don't know," Chike shrugged. "He programmed my parachute to land here, but he went past me jumping, and I was twisting around coming down, completely at the damned thing's mercy. Since you came from uphill, I'm guessing he landed downhill and is working his way back towards us."

"Huh," she said. "Wonder if I can see him from here. Does your radio work? Mine's fried."

"Oh, dear," he replied. "I hadn't thought about that."

Fairchild took a long stride past Chike, planted a foot, and hop-ran up the side of the little rise. She saw Chike reach up and key his radio manually as she did.

She grinned. That was more like Chike, the slightly-absent-minded-professor type.

His voice kind of faded into the background as she looked down.

Visions of OCD moles with carpentry tools suddenly reared gigantic in her mind as she looked straight down into hell.

Okay, maybe not hell. It wasn't bright red down there. No dancing devils waved at her and invited her to join them. At least, not this time.

The rise was hollow. Rather like a miniature volcano, with a two meter wide hole going down at probably an eighty-degree angle into the earth, deep out of sight in the darkness.

"What the hell…?" she muttered.

The tunnel also went down into the earth at an angle that would intercept the line of the game trail about thirty meters down, give or take.

"What is it, Fairchild?" Chike asked, turning and finding her staring down, mouth probably agape.

She felt him hop up beside her and steady himself by waving both arms comically.

"Lacumaces is almost here," Chike said. "Apparently, my beacon is working fine, even as yours was damaged by the storm. And…Oh, my…"

Even boffins will see things eventually, if you give them time.

The hole in the ground was doubly strange because of the shape. The stones of the pile had been wedged close together, and then set in something. Fairchild had assumed just mud or dirt, but now she wasn't so sure.

The inside of the hole was threaded. That was the word that came to mind. A hole in the middle perhaps two meters across, but it had a spiral shape lip all the way around as if set by God's own wood screw, about half a meter wide itself, bored down into the ground and set with these close stones.

OCD Moles, with carpentry tools. Giant ones.

It could happen, right?

"What in the world is that?" Chike asked.

"Do you know what it reminds me of?" Eleanor asked.

"Who's that?" Chike asked suddenly.

Dani sighed, mostly inside. Normally, the Governess kept a low profile. Certainly, she had never spoken to Chike before this, but Fairchild had only generally dealt with the head boffin over the radio anyway.

She reached up between her breasts and pulled Eleanor out.

"Dr. Chike Odille, Chief Expedition Planetologist, may I introduce you to my Governess, Eleanor," Fairchild said, holding her up. "Eleanor, Dr. Odille."

"Please," he said, unconsciously holding up a hand to shake before he stopped himself. "Call me Chike. I've never met a full AI before."

"Thank you, Chike," Eleanor said.

"What was it you were saying, madame?" Chike asked. "This reminded you of something?"

Fairchild felt like she could disappear, but for holding Eleanor up. That was okay. She didn't need to be the center of attention here.

With a flash of insight, Fairchild wondered if Eleanor was doing this specifically to deflect this boffin. As she had said earlier, an AI couldn't co-author an article in an academic journal, just like she couldn't own real property, or be subject to most laws.

But if the words came out of Eleanor's mouth, and not Fairchild's, Chike might be willing to take all the credit himself. Probably with some pushing on her part, the kind that verged on blackmail.

Chike Odille was far too nice and upstanding to hog the spotlight to himself, but he might be willing to let her stand clear over on the edge of the stage and smile pretty.

Those deportment classes had to serve some purpose in her life, right?

"A puquios," Eleanor said simply.

Fairchild had never heard the term before, but she wasn't plugged directly into an encyclopedia. That was what she had Eleanor for.

"A puquios?" Chike repeated. "But that's impossible. That would suggest it was an air shaft down to a man-made, underground water tunnel. There's nothing like that around here."

Lady Danielle Cooper wanted to remain perfectly silent and still. Pretty, decorative, pliable. The kind of woman Alphonse Cooper preferred.

It would be so easy to do right now.

Even easier than pulling out the Tomya and putting a few kilograms of pressure on a trigger.

But she couldn't do that.

Lady Danielle Cooper would actively encourage Chike

Odille to take all the credit. Just hide and make everyone else do the work, and clean up the mess.

Eleanor was covering for her, so she didn't have to stand up for herself and say something.

Like the woman always had.

How many decades had Dani been hiding behind Eleanor's skirts?

Enough.

In her mind, Fairchild growled defiance.

It sounded remarkably like the call of a giant raptor.

Fairchild's Golden Eagle, perhaps.

"It's an airshaft to a qanat, Dr. Odille," Fairchild's voice shattered the calm, afternoon air. "The path we've been following for the last several hours runs above it. The line is as straight as a surveyor could run it, following the general slope of the mountains in perfectly straight lines."

If she hadn't been paying such close attention, Fairchild would have never seen the difference. A white person like Fairchild was technically normally pink in hue, and would fade to alabaster as all the blood drained out of their face.

Chike turned a kind of dark umber, but the reason was the same.

"Do you have any idea of the implications of what you just said, Fairchild?" he whispered intently.

She wanted to shrug. Maybe slouch. Slink off into the Trudywood trees and hide. Climb into the bottle and pull the worm in with her.

Yesterday, she would have.

Today, she had considered using the Tomya to make it all go away.

But that was Lady Danielle Cooper, a flouncing, bubbling airhead of a bimbo that wanted nothing more than the latest adrenaline rush, the latest extreme sports fad. The latest, mindless drivel.

Anything to fill that bottomless emptiness.

But Fairchild was a-borne, a navy-blue Golden Eagle in the skies of Escudra VI.

"Yes, I do, Dr. Odille," she replied calmly, staring the man in the eyes and daring him to do his worst. "Eleanor and I have spent the last several hours discussing the topic and exploring the possibilities."

She could see herself now, standing in front of a room filled with boffins-in-training and reporters, lecturing with one of those long, birch pointer rods they always had in period movies with stuffy professors.

In her mind, she was stark naked as she did so.

And the nakedness didn't bother her.

"Dr. Odille?" another voice yelled. "Are you here?"

"Lacumaces," Chike smiled. He turned, raising a hand to wave.

The boffin started to say something else, but a tremendous crack and rumble overrode his words as the ground shifted and started to fall away, down and into the hole beneath their feet.

Fairchild threw herself backwards and to one side, the instinct of an aeronaut drilled so deep into her soul that even unconscious reflex was slow by comparison.

Her last glimpse of Chike's face was one of utter surprise, followed just as suddenly by the kind of utter, relaxed calm she had felt at that moment when that storm had turned ugly.

And then he was gone into the earth.

CHAPTER TWENTY-TWO

CHIKE

ONE MOMENT, everything was good.

Chike had found Fairchild. Lacumaces was just about to join them. They were all set to get to a place where they could get back to Calypso-2 and return to Ground Station Beta like conquering heroes.

The next, catastrophe. Or, rather, gravity.

The geologist in his soul recognized the sound before his brain even processed that there was a sound to be concerned about.

Mortar crumbling.

Perhaps it would be better to say the mortar had long since rotted and crumbled, and the stones were held in place by inertia and mass. Having stayed in place in spite of wind and weather for however many years (Centuries? Millennia?), they were all set to remain.

Until a pudgy, middle-aged Professor of Planetology stood atop them and shifted his weight in the process of turning, pushing rocks that had been stable to move sideways and press against each other instead of their downstairs neighbors.

Of course they had taken offense. It was the nature of rocks to do that. Given any excuse, they would fail to hold you upright, grasping with greedy fingers to pull you down steep slopes, hoping to bury you at the bottom when they could assemble a whole army of little rocks, like ants, to do the trick.

All that, in the blink of an eye.

The geologist nodded approvingly as Fairchild threw herself clear from one awkwardly-balanced foot. She was a bird. That was natural.

He was a scholar. They didn't move nearly as quickly.

But Fairchild and Lacumaces were both here. They would be able to handle anything this angry planet chose to throw at them, no matter how much trouble he had gotten himself into with the rocks below.

He felt like that character in the children's cartoon who ran three meters past the edge of the cliff and hung in air until they could turn to the camera and make a silly, surprised face.

Chike felt gravity take hold of him.

Freefall.

Darkness.

Somewhere in his soul an adventurer awoke from a decades-long slumber. Perhaps grad school, filled with crazy stunts and the sorts of juvenile hijinks generally frowned upon by faculty members and the local gendarme.

The scholar was lost, in over his head literally as well as figuratively.

Chike tried to relax, but freefall took him into a steep embankment with a lip that caught his foot.

Before he could react, the weight of his belly and chest had tumbled him over forward, like those first seconds outbound from the shuttle.

The scholar identified the lip as part of what Eleanor had

called the puquios, corkscrewing down into the earth for reasons he could not understand.

Not yet. There would be an answer. He just had to demand it. That would come.

The slope remained there. Not quite straight down, but not shallow enough to catch him. Chike brushed stone again, this time with a gloved hand and a shoulder.

The helmet absorbed the blow. It probably would have cracked his skull, had he been doing this later enough in the day to have taken the helmet off.

Chike didn't even know how to do that, to pop the emergency helmet off and breathe the local air. He had been relying on Lacumaces to push the right button.

Fairchild probably knew as well.

If he was going to turn into an adventurer, it was obvious to Chike that there were going to be evenings and weekends spent with much younger folks learning these things.

Otherwise, he might not survive being an adventurer.

And that just wouldn't do.

Still, he saw stars, circling just like the cartoon character always saw. Maybe there was something there, after all.

Chike was amazed at how rational he was able to follow all the happenings as he fell into a deep hole in the earth.

Feet and knees touched another ring as he fell. They were getting closer together, or he was falling faster.

Gravity won that argument.

He felt himself spin again, friction rubbing his side against another rock in the darkness.

The next blow was square against his face-plate.

Light.

Darkness.

CHAPTER TWENTY-THREE

FAIRCHILD

FAIRCHILD COULDN'T HAVE EVEN TOLD Eleanor where the image in her head came from. Probably a geology lecture at some point.

Fairchild certainly wasn't the type of person who read books for pleasure.

It had been the regularity of the clearings, like metronomes, that had planted the thought in her head, lonely as it might have been in there. Seeing the little hill with the hole in the middle just crystalized it in her head.

Fairchild didn't know the work puquios, but she knew what a qanat was. Knew they had been common in the ancient days. Dig a shaft straight down into the ground atop a hill or mountain until you hit the water table. Go a little deeper to be sure, and then start boring sideways at a very slight incline until you emerged from the side of the mountain, remembering to drop vertical shafts for maintenance and air at regular intervals.

That was the key. Regular intervals.

As regular as the ticks of a metronome clicking away atop the piano you were learning to play.

At the bottom of the mountain, you will have created an underground aqueduct.

Fairchild could remember seeing something like that in Spain that the Romans had built, however many centuries ago, that still supplied water to a city.

She refused to even think about what this thing below her was, or how it had gotten there.

Giant, OCD Moles with carpentry tools.

Why was a question for the boffins to answer tomorrow. Right now, Chike was in trouble and there was nobody else who could save him.

In her mind, little Dani wanted to say something, but Fairchild interrupted her with a savage snarl.

He came for you. You're going for him. I don't care how scared you are. I don't care how dark it is, or cold, or cramped. Owls roost in the ground and they aren't afraid.

After that, the voice was silent.

Fairchild was on her feet by then, standing as close to the newly-broken edge of the lip as she dared.

She would dare more, shortly, but she needed to plan.

She turned and located Lacumaces, sprinting across the clearing towards her.

Fairchild held up a hand and waved it.

"Hold there," she commanded.

Lacumaces looked like he wanted to argue with her. Maybe pull rank as the resident Search and Rescue expert.

After all, wasn't he here to rescue her in the first place?

Dani might have allowed it. Probably welcomed someone else taking charge and doing all the hard thinking.

Lacumaces had the right instincts, most of the time.

Right now, it would get both him and Chike killed.

"I said stop, damn it," she snarled at him.

That seemed to get through.

"What?" he asked, coming to a rest at the foot of her little rise.

Up close, the man looked generically Mediterranean, much darker than her, but not nearly Chike's color. Straight black hair. Hooked nose.

Cute, but a total freaking rush junkie.

Fairchild had gotten over the need to push things to the edge of death for fun.

She pointed down at the mound.

"This is an airshaft," she said. Let him worry later about the what and the how of her knowing. It felt right. "Chike was standing here when the ground gave way under his feet."

"Right," Lacumaces said, staring to pull his pack clear.

"You aren't going down the hole, Lacumaces," Fairchild said in a hard voice. "I am."

"Damn it, Fairchild," the man's face curled up in a sneer. "We're here to rescue you."

"I know that," she countered. "My radio's already hosed. Yours wouldn't work underground, anyway, and I need you to keep in touch with Rain and Ann-Marta. That means you stay here and provide me backup. But you're going to have to move to stay ahead of us."

"What?" he asked, confused.

Good, she had his attention. She jumped clear of the rise and led him to the path, using her arm again to point out how straight it was in both directions.

"This follows an underground aqueduct," she said. "It's flowing downhill, but I don't know how fast, or how deep, and I won't until I get to the bottom and look around. We don't have the equipment to pull either of us back to the surface, so we may have to follow it all the way to the bottom and see where it comes out."

Fairchild realized that there was too much to explain. Chike might be drowning or dying in the qanat while she tried to overcome her own reticence to explain things to someone with a brain like Lacumaces.

Inspiration struck. It was almost painful.

"I'm going to leave Eleanor with you," Fairchild said, handing the Aide into Lacumaces hands.

"Eleanor," she continued. "You explain everything to him and anyone else that asks."

"That I will," Eleanor replied as Fairchild turned and jogged across the grass. "Good luck, Fairchild."

She paused once to glance down into a cold, wet hell and take a breath. She quickly re-attached her flight membranes, checked her life support dials, and lit up the twin, ram's horn headlights.

Darkness.

Wet, dark walls broken up by the way the hole was augured into the stone. Maybe seventy-five degrees, now that she was thinking in freefall mode.

Screw you.

Fairchild stepped into nothing.

There wasn't space to really glide in here. But she didn't need speed. If anything, she would have liked to pull a stunt like this with a proper parachute, the kind that would drop her more or less straight.

She settled for puffing herself up like a thistle and letting her surface area piston as much air as possible down in front of her. Fairchild knew she was right about the tunnel system when she fell.

If this was just a well, the air wouldn't have anywhere to escape as she fell, so it would compress and slow her down until it could slip by her fringes. But this was rushing along with her, so it had somewhere to go.

This was another new sport she could invent when she got back to civilization. Add a timer and rules about touching the walls, and see how long you could stay up.

The free-glider slowed her some as she intended, and she kept her weight as far back as she could. As a result, she had to occasionally butt her head forward to push off a wall, but more frequently she would touch with her feet, run a step or two and then hop to clear that next lip.

It was like rappelling face-first down a mine shaft.

She could see the bottom rushing up at her now.

Instinct made her want to curl into a cannon ball when she hit, but she had no idea how deep the water was. She braced herself instead, arms and legs as far apart as she could get, willing herself to stall in the tight confines of the tube as it widened out.

Fairchild clenched her jaw and neck to reduce the risk of a concussion. The water was a black pool, welcoming her into death.

Before, that might have been an easy way to go. Just let the water claim her.

Before, she might have even been willing.

Impact.

Pain.

Water.

Fairchild could see underwater. Those twin lights were brutally powerful.

She could breathe, never having undone the faceplate or life support, intent on finding water on a dry planet before she did anything stupid, like get naked and enjoy the warm sun on her skin.

The current wasn't even that bad. Clear water, flowing at barely a walking pace, as near as she could tell without all of her electronic systems to back up her guesses.

Fairchild detached her flight membranes again, turning back into a person and not a flying squirrel.

She needed to become a mermaid, so she left the one

between her legs. That would give her an amazing dolphin kick.

The water here was around three meters deep, and the smooth sides were seven or eight meters apart.

She could see a lip running along both sides. She would have said catwalk, but it was too narrow, even for elite fashion models. You would need to be a cat to walk on something less than half a meter wide, slick, and sloped in ever so slightly.

Whoever built this was skinny and amazingly sure-footed.

She wondered if her OCD Moles with carpentry tools really were giant boring machines. Qanats could be cut by hand, and had been in antiquity, but this was something on an entirely different scale from those claustrophobic tunnels she remembered from a picture book somewhere.

At least the current was clear and her suit insulated. She could only imagine how cold that damned water would be, coming up from the water table itself.

And Chike didn't have any insulation.

Well, a small beer belly, but hypothermia would be setting in quickly in this environment.

Fairchild started to swim hard, digging with her hands and kicking with her powerful legs, as if she could outrun the river itself to sunlight.

CHAPTER TWENTY-FOUR

CHIKE

IT WAS the cold that brought him to his senses.

Chike had thrown off the covers while he slept and was now too cold to stay asleep.

But he couldn't find them when he reached to pull those covers back up.

Floating.

That wasn't right.

He opened his eyes. At least he thought he did.

The darkness didn't change.

The cold was bone deep. It was becoming painful.

Chike splashed his hands out of the water.

Water?

Water. Cold water, seeping into his boots, his belt, and his wrists. Already, his core temperature was dropping.

Where the hell was he?

Escudra VI. Puquios. Landslide.

Things flashed back suddenly.

Falling. Tumbling. Blackout.

Now he was in an underground river. That was what

Fairchild had said. She had been following a man-made artifact above ground that she thought was an aqueduct.

Why hadn't he drowned when he fell in?

He was floating upright. How was that possible?

And he could breathe.

Helmet. Emergency suit to jump out of a Survey Shuttle named Calypso-2.

Chike's brains felt like they had rattled loose in his skull. He wondered if this was what it felt like to have suffered a concussion. Certainly, everything was muddled.

More muddled than normal for him.

He was in an underground river, floating along on the current, and he was so cold that it hurt.

He was also in an emergency suit.

"Helmet, lights on, please," he said out loud, hoping that the onboard system was smart enough to overcome a dumb user.

A single beam of light suddenly lit in the middle of his forehead, like a unicorn fish.

The walls were smooth, but he could see where stones had been cut to shape and set.

The suit was holding him upright. Apparently, there was one of those automated inflation devices, like aircraft and ground-to-orbit shuttles were always carrying on about, during the pre-flight safety lecture everybody ignored. It was holding his head above water, and letting his feet drag below him in the current.

But it was still damned cold.

Chike turned his unicorn helmet to the sides, trying to figure out how he could escape the water before hypothermia set in and he was too weak to move.

Lacumaces was up above. Fairchild was as well. And Eleanor. It had been delightful to meet a fully sentient AI. Those were so rare.

But it made sense that someone like Lady Danielle Cooper would have one. He would have to figure out a way to let her know that he knew who she was, if only so he could cover for her.

Gods, it was getting hard to think, as well. The cold was leeching into his brains and turning them to molasses.

At least Lacumaces had put him in the suit before the smoke jump. Otherwise, he would have already passed out.

How to use the time he had left?

Chike let the light play on his right. There seemed to be a lip of some sort, like a swimming pool might have.

Ledge, that was the word.

This is getting bad. I need to get warm. Does the suit have any brains, or just the helmet?

"Suit, temperature up, please," he said in a weak voice.

Nothing responded, so he couldn't tell if it didn't understand, or just couldn't do that. Hard to tell.

Chike the Adventurer was going to have to save his own ass, if he wanted out of this alive.

Next week, survival classes that include rapid-water immersion. Maybe I should become a paramedic, while I'm at it.

Chike laughed out loud at the overall silliness of a forty-six-year-old geologist inventing a second life for himself as an adventurer. But hadn't Lacumaces given up being a fabulously-overpaid doctor to live as a Ground Services expert?

You gotta do what's going to make you happy, maybe, instead of what society expects of you.

He could add some adventuring to his life. He was already having more fun and felt more alive that he had in decades.

Okay, first, swim.

Chike's helmet made motion awkward, since it refused to go under water for longer than a moment. He ended up kind of dog-paddling to one side and drawing closer to the lip.

He found the stone to be smooth as it carried him along, unable to hold on to anything before the current ripped his hands loose.

Oh, dear. Growing weaker.

He felt his hands begin to curl into angry, painful, little talons. At least his legs were still warm from all the kicking. But he needed to get out of the water quickly.

Aqueduct. Ancient Roman method of delivering water from the mountains to a city, usually by means of elevated stone platforms that traveled at a very, very gentle slope.

Qanat was an even older technique that dated to ancient Persia, but served the same general principle. Deliver water from a frigid, mountain spring to a city so that you could have agriculture in the desert.

But the ones he remembered were much smaller. Perhaps a few meters wide and barely a meter deep. He would have been able to stand up in one of those and free himself.

This was a monstrous undertaking, delivering a tremendous amount of water somewhere.

And he needed to help his rescuers.

Would it better to try to swim upriver, on the assumption that they would be coming after him, or downriver on the assumption that the faster he got to daylight, the better off he would be?

An adventurer would know this answer. The geologist was stumped.

Chike saw a flash of light above him as he tried to get enough friction to hold himself still against the current.

Skylight.

No, another puquios.

The water was rougher suddenly, almost white and choppy.

Chike realized why the shaft was angled and threaded. It would channel wind down into the tube and help push the water faster.

He also felt a jar as his fingers encountered some sort of flaw in the stone of the walkway.

That made sense, if this was man-made. Or whomever made.

If you came down the shaft, you might want to tie up a boat so you could explore and repair the tunnel.

How far apart were they?

Fairchild had said they were regular, and she had been seeing them without realizing what they signified until she looked down one.

The rest of the roof was smooth, except for the hole near the top on his right as he tried to swim against the current and hold his place.

It was a futile gesture.

But he could work his way downriver, using the exercise to keep his muscles warm, and see if he could catch the next one.

Riding an underground river was nice, but he was cold, miserable, and trapped.

He wanted out.

Now.

CHAPTER TWENTY-FIVE

FAIRCHILD

TIMES LIKE THIS, she really could have used the electronics that had gotten shattered by the face of the mountain last night. Her radio wouldn't punch through thirty meters of rock, but it would have worked just fine down in this tunnel to call Chike and let him know that help was on the way.

Yelling would have required her to open the faceplate and risk sucking in water.

And there was no other way to signal.

Or was there?

Fairchild had her headlights blasting away at the darkness like cutting lasers. She turned down river and looked, but she was too close to the surface of the rough water to see anything.

She could, however, signal him with the lights, if he was awake. Let him know that help was in the tunnel.

Fairchild reached up and blinked her lights three times. Three, the ancient and standard way to indicate distress.

There was no response, but she really didn't expect any. Chike had gotten a long head start from the time he had fallen until she could get Lacumaces to understand the next steps. Then she had glided down the ramp where he had free-fallen.

Call it two minutes, water speed unknown but fast enough to have pushed him forward.

She looked up as she thought, seeing the tunnel without the benefit of Eleanor's brains and encyclopedic memory. Definitely a made-thing, and not the result of gigantic moles. Organic ones, anyway. Although that would have made for an even cooler discovery: Fairchild's Monstrous Moles.

Chike was never going to let her get away with not claiming at least some credit for this discovery. Especially not after she rescued him from it.

She would have to embrace fame. See if she could parley it into fortune, or at least a better flying gig.

Grow up, although she growled angrily at herself and the universe for even suggesting the concept.

Lady Danielle Cooper, that quivering, mewing little airhead who was only useful as an adornment on some man's arm, was going to have to die. Right here, in this darkness. Buried in this wet tomb.

Only Fairchild would be allowed to live.

Or neither of them. Because if she couldn't handle it, there were still ways. But she was never going back to Alphonse Cooper's orbit.

She would die first. That much, she could promise.

Fairchild took a deep breath and let go.

Crying inside a sealed life support environment was a stupid thing to do. She didn't care. The tears squeezed themselves out and splashed off the inside of her faceplate, salty kisses when she opened her mouth to breathe.

Fairchild would survive and none of the rest of them.

Did that mean Eleanor was no longer needed?

Her oldest friend in the world had also been her constant

minder for over twenty-five years. Had she helped keep Dani sane, or retarded her emotionally so that Alphonse Cooper could control his wayward daughter?

So many questions.

Lady Danielle Cooper might have sought answers. Dani would have wanted to know.

Fairchild didn't give a shit.

She was a Golden Eagle, flying the skies of Escudra VI even as she swam the chthonic depths, seeking Pluto.

This was the River Styx. There was a ferryman awaiting his two silver pieces for her soul, somewhere down there.

He couldn't have it.

Not without a fight.

Fairchild was not about to surrender.

A chill came over her soul, starting behind her belly-button and spreading to her limbs before it turned to liquid fire in her veins.

Where had this new demanding bitch come from?

The other bitch had wanted her to surrender, to curl up and die. To not fight any more.

But she was still Alphonse Cooper's daughter in her blood.

Try me, lady.

Fairchild unconsciously took a breath as she dove, even with the life support cocooning her.

She let the rage power her legs as she started a aggressive dolphin kick and pushed herself hard against the water.

Charon might be willing to take Chike's soul down here.

She would just have to fight him for it.

CHAPTER TWENTY-SIX

CHIKE

THE COLD WAS GROWING WORSE. He could feel it seeping in through a gap in the jumpsuit near his waist, into his socks, and around his wrists where the gloves weren't water tight.

Why did a smoke jumper need to be water tight, anyway?

The swimming helped. His legs were tight and stiff, but still moving. He could breathe as he forced himself to dog-paddle down river, working to use every muscle and keep them warm enough that he could try his luck at the next overhead tunnel entrance.

Chike was afraid he had missed the next vertical in the darkness as he swam, the monotony was so great. But he saw it far enough ahead that he could get himself turned sideways and do a long stroke to try and stay even, relative to the water.

It worked, for the most part. He kept bumping his nose against the rock, but he managed to get close and was just barely moving down river at this point.

What he didn't know was how long he could keep it up.

Being an adventurer was requiring way more effort than his forty-six-year-old butt could handle. Add that to the list of things next week. More pushups, more sit-ups, get your lazy bottom out of the chair and do some exercise so you can keep up with these kids.

Otherwise, crap like this might kill you.

Chike counted his too-fast heartbeats and hoped he was close enough. He surged up and got his head above the level of the stone lip.

There. Dark spot. Hopefully nothing is living there. Or at least, hopefully, they aren't venomous.

He stabbed out with his left hand and managed to hook his fingers into the little, recessed dimple. There was a ring or something there. He couldn't tell without climbing out of the water, but that presented its own problem.

The water did not relent in trying to drag him down into the darkness. And there was nothing else to grab onto if he wanted to pull himself out of the water.

And it was cold.

The coldness had seeped all the way into his bones now, worse since he was just hanging on and not swimming.

And now his arm was starting to go to sleep.

But he could see daylight overhead, a Roman-style Oculus letting late-afternoon sun down into his abyss.

Rain was up there somewhere, circling and waiting for a signal. Lacumaces would be along soon and he would have a plan.

But it was cold.

Chike wondered if he should just let go. The waves would try to claim him, but the helmet would keep them at bay, at least for a while.

And if this was an aqueduct, it had to come out somewhere.

Or did, once upon a very long time ago.

What happened to major feats of engineering, when your society has so collapsed that all evidence of your species had vanished?

It was possible that the river never surfaced. Perhaps it just went on underground forever, and he would never make it out. The battery in his unicorn lamp would last for a long time, even after his oxygen had given out.

They would have to send specialist dive teams down to recover his body, assuming that he hadn't been eaten by fish. At least not too badly.

Something caught his eye.

Lights below him nearly made Chike wet himself.

Something was moving beneath the water, and it glowed.

And it was coming closer.

Okay, maybe it was time to pee.

At least that was warm, even as his heart turned to ice.

CHAPTER TWENTY-SEVEN

FAIRCHILD

SO FAR, so good.

The water was almost transparent as Fairchild swam along, letting her life support protect her from what must be glacially-cold temperatures while she looked for Chike's body.

If he had drowned, he would be down here somewhere, floating just below the surface. Bodies didn't start floating until the decay of death caused them to fill up with gas and rise to the surface.

Nothing.

She had not missed him. And she couldn't imagine that he could have gotten himself out of the water.

Briefly, Fairchild considered surfacing, just so she could pop her faceplate and yell once. The tunnel would echo badly, but he would at least know someone was there.

Plus, the headlights would help.

What was that?

Ah, found him.

He'd managed to grab onto something and hold still against the current.

Almost swam right by him.

Fairchild turned her lithe body like an eel and began to dig hard against the water.

It was flowing at barely a walking pace. Implacable, but not impossible. She managed to make good headway, getting a significant distance back before she surfaced.

Wouldn't do to pop up so close she blasted right by him, nor managed to knock him loose from whatever he was holding onto.

Once clear, she turned around and surfaced, somewhere between a submarine probe and a sturgeon.

Quickly, she unlocked her faceplate and opened it. It was fine if she got water inside right now. Her neck was sealed, and the helmet was designed with enough positive pressure and backflow valves that it would empty itself back out quickly.

It was like she had bought the absolute most expensive, top of the line model, or something.

Never jump out of a shuttle with cheap gear.

She wouldn't be able to hold perfectly still, swimming on her side, but it would be close enough to talk.

"Hiya, doc," she called.

"God, I thought you were a shark or something," Chike exhaled back. "Do you have any idea what those lights look like underwater when you move around?"

Nope, but it sounded like yet another interesting sport she could invent when she got home. Or at least back to civilization.

She laughed instead, and accidurally swallowed a mouthful of water. It was pure. Colder than hell, but tasted lovely.

"You okay?" she finally sputtered. "Hold on."

Fairchild took a deep breath, popped her faceplate closed, and dolphin-kicked hard a few times to gain a couple of body lengths before she surfaced and opened her helmet.

"I've got a grommet to hold, or something," Chike yelled as she swam. "But the water's too cold and I can't find a way to get up on the rock."

Fairchild drove herself up in the air, using both legs and the glider membrane hooked to her ankles. She was going to have to build a version of this suit for scuba diving, when she got home. Pretend to be a manta or something, and just freeglide the water. She'd need a stinger tail or something, though. Partly for verisimilitude, partly for protection against large predators sneaking up on her.

More hobbies for Fairchild. Good thing I'm about to become a fashion icon, too. I'll be able to afford more toys.

Inspiration took the form of a shark. She could hear the orchestral music start up in her head so loud she nearly burst out laughing.

"Okay, got a plan," she gasped between kicks as she tried to stay even with the boffin. "Gonna dive, then come up under you and lift you onto the ledge. Your job to stay up."

"Got it," he said. "Hurry, please."

Fairchild got her head fully out of the water and snapped the faceplate closed. She let the current carry her down while she rested. Swimming like this was a tremendous amount of exercise. It felt good, but she could feel her reserves burning now.

All the walking with Eleanor, trying to escape her past, hadn't helped.

Okay. Shark Concerto Number 1. I need to add that music when I fix the helmet.

Fairchild slid beneath the waves and let the water take over. She dove to the bottom of the qanat and touched the smooth stone. It would do. Not great, but not icy slick either.

She could work with this.

Forward now, the water was flowing slower at depth than the surface. Probably something to do with the airshafts letting wind in to push the water.

Whatever it was, as long as she stayed low, she could swim easier against it. Not much, but enough that she could position herself like an eel down in the rocks.

Fairchild centered on Chike's legs and surged upright, driving off the bottom like all the world depended on it.

She caught the boffin by the butt and dolphin-kicked as hard as she could. She felt him tense, and then grow feather-light as she got him out of the current and into the air.

God, that hurt.

Fairchild felt all her muscles clench and strain. She rolled over onto her side and kicked to fight the current as best she could.

Chike was flat on his side, butt back against the wall facing out. One arm still had a death-grip into the hole, so whatever was there was solid.

That would keep him in place until help arrived.

He could sit up when he got warm, and stand if he was careful.

Now, to get them here quickly.

Fairchild pushed herself one last time to get up-current from Chike. She turned and let her feet precede her, popping her helmet open so she could talk to the man.

He was blowing like he had just run a marathon, but this was a boffin. They weren't supposed to be in shape.

Still, she could save the man. He had saved her, after all.

They all had.

Fairchild pulled the Tomya from her hip holster and held it up. Still set on emergency flare launcher. Safety on.

All set.

She got close to the ledge and yelled.

"Chike, take this," and slid the survival tool onto the shelf next to his hand.

She felt him try to grab her hand, but she twisted free and left him with only the gun instead.

"Point it up the shaft and fire," she yelled as she was past him. She turned and let the current carry her. They could hold a conversation without screaming, while the water pushed her farther. "You've got three more flares."

"Damn it, Fairchild," Chike yelled back. "What about you?"

Fairchild felt her shoulders shrug. Lady Danielle Cooper would be a quivering mass of panic right now. Dani would be trying to hide.

Fairchild wasn't afraid.

"I want to see where it comes out," she called. "After Lacumaces and Rain get you up, come find me at the bottom."

"What if it never comes out?" Chike pleaded with her.

"There are risks in life, Doc," she said. "Some of them are worth taking, for friends. Thank you for showing me that, and coming for me. And tell Eleanor I made it. She'll understand."

Fairchild popped her faceplate closed and dove at that point.

Chike would be fine, up and out of the water where he could get dry. One quick flare and the cavalry would be there in minutes.

But the darkness beckoned her, promising her the secrets of Escudra VI, and maybe Charon as well.

But that the price she was willing to pay.

CHAPTER TWENTY-EIGHT

CHIKE

CHIKE DIDN'T PARTICULARLY like doing press conferences. And it didn't feel right, standing alone at the edge of the stage waiting, but he had no choice. It was just him to face all those people.

He told himself it would be just like a lecture hall, only one where the students were awake and actually sober this morning. Probably.

The lectern was all set up, with a microphone already adjusted to his height. Out there, a sea of reporters with camera, notepads, slabs, and smiles like sharks.

And he had to face them alone.

Still, it was possibly the most important archaeological discovery since Heinrich Schliemann identified Troy. And if a simple geologist had to steal the thunder of the rest of human science, that was their own damned fault for being late to the game.

Escudra VI had been inhabited.

Nobody knew how long ago, but there had been people there, of some sort. And nobody could yet answer why they had left, or where they had gone, but they had left behind fingerprints.

Maybe they were in a hurry. Maybe something had happened, but they had created a swamp at the base of a mountain, either accidentally when eternity intruded or for purposes mankind had not yet fathomed.

He would leave that to the hydrologists to argue over. After all, he had been there first.

Chike's patience wore out and he gave up waiting.

He tugged the unfamiliar tie a bit and hitched up his slacks. The last notch on his belt was barely enough today, but he had lost eight kilos in the last three months.

It would be time to treat himself to a new wardrobe for Christmas.

Chike stepped out on stage to a sudden round of thunderous applause that caused him to stutter a step. Students were never excited to participate in a lecture. Something else different he would have to adjust to.

He reached the lectern and picked up the little clicker remote that would cycle through holograms behind him as he spoke.

It was wrong, standing up here alone, when so much of the glory was shared with Fairchild. Eleanor had flat refused any credit and threatened to sick Alphonse Cooper's lawyers on him, but Fairchild could not be left out.

"Good morning, ladies and gentlemen of the press," he said, working his diaphragm to push the sound across the whole auditorium. "I am Dr. Chike Odille, of Michigan State University, and I would like to share with you some of the recent discoveries on the planet Escudra VI."

He paused to take a breath and concentrate.

The lights were high enough to see, but low enough to make the hologram behind him stand out at it transformed from a Spartan logo to a map of the Escudra system. Several photographers took that moment to all fire off their camera flashes, blinding him.

They also revealed a face that had been hidden down in the darkness, smiling wryly up at him with the most wicked gleam.

She had been like that since Escudra VI.

Ann-Marta had noticed it. So had several others. Eleanor had refused to elaborate.

But it didn't matter. She was here.

Chike had been afraid she would skip the press conference completely and be found in her room later, drunk out of her mind.

But she had also stopped drinking since Escudra VI.

It was like a completely different woman had come back than the one who flew into that storm.

"And I would also like to introduce my collaborator," he said, pointing and smiling. "Ladies and gentlemen, the real explorer and adventurer of Escudra VI. Fairchild."

She rose from her chair on the second row aisle and utterly beamed at him. She was dressed in a conservative suit today, dark blue or gray, it was hard to tell without better lighting. Blazer over an open-necked, button-up shirt that appeared to be rose colored, or maybe salmon. She even had a kerchief popped out of her breast pocket, providing a peacock background for Eleanor. Jewelry. Fingernail polish.

Wow.

Fairchild stepped to the edge of the stage and hopped up in one bounce, like a cat climbing into a window.

Chike watched her turn and take the measure of the crowd with a calm, critical eye and that same, wry smile, as if every single person down there was naked and painted blue.

"That's it?" a voice called from the darkness. "Just Fairchild?"

"That's right," he heard her say. "Fairchild."

ABOUT THE AUTHOR

Blaze Ward writes science fiction in the Alexandria Station universe (Jessica Keller, The Science Officer, The Story Road, etc.) as well as several other science fiction universes, such as Star Dragon, the Dominion, and more. He also writes odd bits of high fantasy with swords and orcs. In addition, he is the Editor and Publisher of *Boundary Shock Quarterly Magazine*. You can find out more at his website www.blazeward.com, as well as Facebook, Goodreads, and other places.

Blaze's works are available as ebooks, paper, and audio, and can be found at a variety of online vendors. His newsletter comes out regularly, and you can also follow his blog on his website. He really enjoys interacting with fans, and looks forward to any and all questions—even ones about his books!

Never miss a release!
If you'd like to be notified of new releases, sign up for my newsletter.

http://www.blazeward.com/newsletter/

Buy More!
Did you know that you can buy directly from my website?

https://www.blazeward.com/shop/

Connect with Blaze!

Web: www.blazeward.com
Boundary Shock Quarterly (BSQ):
https://www.boundaryshockquarterly.com/

ABOUT KNOTTED ROAD PRESS

Knotted Road Press fiction specializes in dynamic writing set in mysterious, exotic locations.

Knotted Road Press non–fiction publishes autobiographies, business books, cookbooks, and how–to books with unique voices.

Knotted Road Press creates DRM–free ebooks as well as high–quality print books for readers around the world.

With authors in a variety of genres including literary, poetry, mystery, fantasy, and science fiction, Knotted Road Press has something for everyone.

Knotted Road Press
www.KnottedRoadPress.com

www.ingramcontent.com/pod-product-compliance
Lightning Source LLC
Chambersburg PA
CBHW070534100726
47907CB00004B/1112